CAGED FEAR

CAGED DUET, BOOK 2

NANCY CHASTAIN

Copyright © 2022 by Author Nancy Chastain All rights reserved. No part of this publication may be reproduced, distributed, or transmitted in any form or by any means, including photocopying, recording, or other electronic or mechanical methods, without the prior written permission of the publisher, except in the case of brief quotations embodied in critical reviews and certain other noncommercial uses permitted by copyright law. This book is licensed for your enjoyment only.

The one thing about being an Author you can always count on is someone asking to be in a book. Some bug the hell out of you about it over a long period of time.

There is one individual that has been after me for a while to be in a story. He thought he could decide how he would be portrayed and all his characteristics, but that isn't how it works being friends with an author, especially this author.

I'm the type of person that believes in everyone lives their own life, loves who they love, and color is just that— a color. I'm dedicating this book to everyone out there that has been lucky enough to find their person and the person they want to be.

To everyone that believes all people should be treated equally and with respect no matter their color, sex and religion, may you find all the joy and happiness you seek in this world.

To the rest of you, well… fuck off.

Editing by Dr. Plot Twist.

Cover by Touch Creations Designs.

PROLOGUE

MIKE

Today should have been a day to celebrate. Most of the Hell's Guardians are in jail, the rest dead. More importantly, Jack is dead thanks to me. I shot him, but not before he put some lead in my sister.

I have no clue if she survived, just that my heart stopped when her body collapsed to the ground. The time between the rounds came and went as a blur. I vaguely recall the paramedics rushing around and rolling her toward the ambulance.

Now I'm in my truck, numbly speeding behind the flashing lights until the ambulance comes to a full stop. Flashes of my parents' deaths flood me as the vehicle's back doors swing open. The wheels of the gurney hit the asphalt, slinking and shaking the body that isn't moving.

Macy's body. My blood. All I have left.

Glued to my seat. Ass to the damn leather. I can't get my foot to release the brake or hit the accelerator.

It takes too damn long to get the courage to park and find my way to the waiting room. David greets me with his fist to my face, blaming me for not protecting the woman he loves, my sister. Finding out where away Jack held Macy while blackmailing her and David wasn't enough. I unwillingly walked her into the path of a bullet.

Being hit by someone I respect, who blames me for the same act I blame myself for is torture. It's validation that I deserve what I'm feeling.

That night, I allow myself to do something I've never done before: purchase methamphetamine to dull the pain of the guilt. After doing a couple of lines, I go to a bar to see what other kind of distraction I could find.

I don't expect to see the fiery petite redhead Rosie, my sister's best friend, sitting at the bar drowning her sorrow. I take the bar stool next to her and order us both a beer.

We begin to talk about everything that has happened over the last few years. Three hours later when the bar is ready to close, neither one of us is ready to for the evening to end. Rosie invites me back to her place. Neither one of have any business driving so we hail a cab to keep the night going.

It is easy to connect with Rosie. She loves the same people I do. She has watched them go through the same torment to be together that I have, and she has almost lost them tonight, like me.

No words are needed once the door is closed to the outside world. The only thing that matters is the two of us, and the need to forget, the need to feel anything other than the fear that crippled our lives today. We need to feel, something good, something raw, something new filled with excitement.

There is no taking it slow.

Our lips lock onto each other, and clothing comes off. The only time our kisses break is to remove another piece of clothing.

Tonight, is not about emotion it's about need. About control.

When our bare skin touches, sparks ignite along my skin. Anytime my fingers roam over her body, my nerve endings tingle as if electricity licks at their tips. I've never had such a reaction to a woman.

Our bodies fit together as if molded to be one. I've never had such a natural chemistry with anyone. There is no nervousness with each other.

As I enter her body for the first time, it's as if I have found heaven. In one slow push, Rosie opens to accept every inch of me. She matches me stroke for stroke.

I flip us over to where Rosie is on top riding me. She takes ahold of my forearms, raising up on her knees, then sinking deeply down on to my cock burying me deep. My hands grip her hips, helping her lift up and gently pushing her back down.

Rosie's body quivers as she approaches her peak. We both release together.

The last few hours disappear, and the only thing that matters in the world is the two of us.

Rosie collapses on my chest. I pull a sheet over the two of us, wrapping my arms around her holding her tightly against my chest. Selfishly not wanting to release the wonderful feeling that has replaced the stress of the day.

* * *

I wake in the morning with red hair across my chest. I gently move the hair off to the side, and there lying in my arms is the most beautiful woman I've ever seen. The night before comes flooding my mind. I'm filled with regret. Not regret that it happened, but simply regret how it happened.

Rosie is the type of woman that deserves to be taken out, shown off and slowly and respectfully dated until she is ready to give herself to you. I know she wasn't forced into last night, but I'm not ready to love someone like her.

Not when I can't love myself.

CHAPTER ONE

MIKE

"Hi, I'm Mike. I'm an addict." I stand in front of a group of strangers and admit.

"Hi, Mike," the group responds in unison.

Standing at the podium, I think on what to say next. "I began using while I was undercover. It started as testing the product and continued from there. I figured I could stop anytime, but dealing with the stress of the job and blaming myself for my sister getting shot has proven that I don't have the strength to quit on my own... I'm three days clean and struggling. Thank you for listening."

Once I recognized the problem, I went to my superiors and asked for help before the addiction cost someone their life.

While I undergo treatment, I'm off active duty. I have to see a therapist and attend Narcotics Anonymous for three months, then I'll be reevaluated.

The Oklahoma City Narcotics Division has been my home since I was pulled from the academy and given specialized training due to my family's connections with the Hells Guardians.

Marcus worked and died because of them. After his death, Macy began to dance for them, and I was brought in to handle the drug deals. My dysfunctional family allowed me to become a cop and drug addict without anyone in my life knowing or caring.

The job helped me get revenge and bring the Guardians to justice, but it ended up breaking me. I just have to find the strength to beat this.

I walk to the back of the room and take a seat. A couple of moments later, a familiar face walks up and sits down next to me. "That was some share you gave."

"What are you doing here?" I look at Rosie, my sister's best friend and the manager of Macy's Tattoo Shop. I flash back to that night over a year ago, the one the two of us spent together. We haven't seen each other since then; I've been undercover most of the time, but that doesn't mean I haven't thought of her. Hell, I haven't stopped thinking of her, if I'm being honest with myself.

"For a detective, you're not real smart, are you?" she asks, bumping me in the arm.

"I mean, I didn't know you... How long have you been clean?"

"Four years and eight months," Rosie answers.

"Does Macy know?" I ask her.

"Of course, Macy is the one that brought me to my first meeting. When I didn't want to come, she dragged my ass here and stayed with me to make sure I didn't take off," Rosie replies. "Have you talked to her?"

I don't answer; I just shake my head.

"Why not? Macy and David are the two people that would be there for you through it all."

"I don't know if I can face them."

Rosie takes my hand in hers. "Do you want me to come with you when you tell them?"

"Why would you do that?" I swivel around to look at her. "You haven't seen me in a year."

"If there is one thing this program is going to teach you, Mike, it's that there is no judgement here. We help each other overcome our demons." She squeezes my hand. "Macy was there when I needed someone the most, and I'm going to be here for you."

In the past, anytime anyone had made a statement like that to me, I'd always overanalyze. *What's in it for them? What do they want?*

For the first time, I don't think Rosie is up to anything. I actually believe her when she says I can count on her. I'm not sure what is different about her, compared to anyone else I have ever known, I just believe there is something.

The meeting continues for another thirty minutes as several others stand at the podium and share part of their story. By the end, I realize none of us are that different. We all turned our lives upside down while trying to deal with our demons. Some of us destroyed others' lives in the process, some destroyed their own marriages and families, but being here, we all have one goal in common: overcome our addictions and to try to find ourselves in the process.

Rosie waits on me to get my verification card signed by the meeting organizer. The card is so I can prove to my therapist that I'm attending my meetings as required.

"How do you feel?" she asks me.

"Raw."

"Your night is not over. Come on, we'll take my truck," she tells me and walks off.

"Hey." I jog to catch up with her. "Where exactly are we going?"

She stops in front of a dark purple SSR pickup and opens the driver's door. "We are going to see Macy and David."

I stop with my hand on the door handle. "Rosie, uhm…"

She walks around to the passenger side and stands in front of me. "You can do this. I'll be with you the entire time. Macy loves you and David has forgiven you."

I nod my head as I get in the truck.

Rosie walks around to climb into the driver's seat. "What do you think of my baby?" she asks, wiping off the dash.

"It's a nice truck. How long have you had her?"

"I bought her on my third anniversary of being sober. I knew then I was going to make it. I found it on the Internet. Marcus went with me to make sure I didn't get ripped off. He helped me get her running good and even sent me to a friend of his to get the interior done and painted. I did the mural on the back cover myself. The guys clear coated it for me."

"I had no idea." I look out the window, realizing I really had no clue what my siblings were up to back then. I was lost in my own world, not caring what was going on around me. Marcus and Macy were doing good for others while I played video games only interested in being a kid. How am I supposed to tell Macy after everything she and David have gone through to be together that I'm an addict?

We pull into the driveway of my childhood home. Memories flood my mind: Marcus making sure Macy and I got to school every day. We had to have homework done before we did anything else. He and David were at every football game, every school event. Marcus took over after our parents died, and he killed when some guy tried to rape Macy on her birthday. David sacrificed ten years of his life to keep Marcus out of jail. What did I do?

Rosie places her hand on my arm, bringing me back from my memories. "This is a safe place, Mike. The people in there are your family. I'll be right there with you." She shuts off the truck. "You can do this."

"You're right." I open the truck door and step out. Rosie walks beside me as we head up the sidewalk.

The front door opens before we have a chance to ring the doorbell. "Hey, you two, come on in." Macy steps aside, letting us in before giving us a hug. "David's in the kitchen; he is cooking spaghetti. I hope you are hungry."

I look at Rosie, confused.

"I called Macy and told her we were coming by while I waited on you to come out," she whispers to me.

We enter the kitchen as David drains the pasta. "Hey guys, you're just in time. Have a seat; we'll eat in just a minute."

I take a seat at the table as Macy and David join us, carrying the food. "I'll get the iced tea." Rosie walks to the fridge, returning with a pitcher of tea.

I take a bite of spaghetti, surprised how good it is. "This is really good." I take another bite.

"I'm glad you like it. What have you two been up to this evening?" David asks with a grin.

Macy reaches over and smacks his arm.

Under the table, Rosie places her hand on my thigh and gives me a reassuring squeeze.

I take her hand in mine for support. Placing my fork on my plate, I take a drink of my tea, stalling as much as possible before telling my secret. "I ran into Rosie at a NA meeting."

"We're you there dropping someone off?" Macy asks.

I look to Rosie for a show of support. She nods her head for me to continue. "I have to attend a meeting every day for three months or I'm off the force. I'm an addict."

Macy's eyes fill with tears and my heart breaks that I let her down. Without saying a word, she stands and comes around the table to me. I stand in front of her, prepared to hear her anger and disappointment. Instead, she wraps her arms around my neck and pulls me in close. "Whatever you need, we are here for you."

Knowing I'm not alone in my recovery is a huge relief. "I'm sorry to disappoint you both."

David walks up to me as Macy lets my neck go. "Mike, anything you need, just let me know. We got you." He pulls me into a bear hug. "Day or night, we are here."

"Thank you, both. I really don't know what to say." My body is shaking. I'm not sure if it's from relief or needing a fix.

Rosie takes my hand, helping me to sit down. "Give it a minute, the shakes will pass," she assures me.

Macy gets up from the table and goes to the refrigerator. She comes back with a glass of orange juice. "Here, drink this. When is the last time you had something in your stomach?"

"I had a sandwich yesterday. I'm not that hungry."

"You have to eat. Take your time and eat some more spaghetti," Macy urges me.

I nod my head in agreement, setting down the glass and taking a bite of the food.

The conversation turns toward what is going on at the tattoo shop and how things are going at the gym.

Macy and Rosie move to the living room after everyone is done eating while I help David clean up the kitchen and load the dishwasher.

I start to head into the other room when David puts his hand on my shoulder. "Can we talk for a moment?"

"Sure." I lean against the counter, waiting to hear what he has to say.

"I have an idea I would like to run by you. Just bear with me for a minute. I go to the gym every morning at four a.m. to work out before we open, and I'm there until we close. Why don't you stay here with us and come with me?"

"Naw, I don't want to put you guys out. You don't want me hanging around. Thanks for the offer, but I'll be fine." I push away from the counter and start to walk off.

"Mike, I'm not feeling sorry for you. You're not fine. You are family. I hope you will start thinking of me that way one day. You being alone is not the answer." He stands in front of me.

"You need to stay busy and out of your head. Just give it a try for a few days. If it doesn't help, we'll try something else." He just stands there looking at me. "Besides, you got somewhere else to be?"

"You know I don't."

"Good. Then it's settled. Let's tell Macy and Rosie we are going to go to your place and pick up some of your stuff."

"You're going to be a pain in my ass, aren't you?" I ask him. I can't help grinning; he reminds me of Marcus.

"Yep." He pats me on the shoulder as he walks out of the kitchen toward the girls, who are laughing.

The girls quit talking when we enter the room. David announces we are going to go to my place and get some stuff and what the next few days are going to include.

Macy voices her approval while Rosie watches me. "Hey, Mike. You good with all this?"

What am I supposed to say? *Fuck no! I want everyone to leave me the fuck alone.* "It will work out fine. I can't sit around and do nothing all day."

"Let me see your phone." Rosie stands and walks to me with her hand out. "Here's my number. When things get rough, call me. I'll pick you up for the meeting tomorrow." She calls her phone, so she has my number without even asking.

"Are you sure that won't be a problem?"

"No problem. I told you I'm going to be there for you."

"Thanks Rosie. I'll see you tomorrow," I say as David, and I get in his car. I give him directions to where I have been staying.

The ride to the apartment I used while undercover is quiet.

It was nice not having to fill every second with conversation. As I open the door, the familiar need fills my body. I shake as the urge for my next line of meth hits me hard. I lean against the refrigerator to keep from falling to the floor.

David grabs my arm and helps me to a chair. "You did most of it when you were here, didn't you? There is no way in hell you can stay here. Do you have any drugs stashed away?"

I don't answer him. I put my head on the table, hoping the room will quit spinning.

"Mike..." David jerks me up by my arm. "Do you have any drugs here?"

I pull away from him. "In the fucking bathroom cabinet. It's not like I was fucking going in there to do it!" I yell at him.

David goes down the hall and comes back with the familiar box that I kept my drugs and paraphernalia in. He turns on the water in the sink and the garbage disposal.

I try to remain calm, knowing what he is about to do, but I can't fake my reaction as he dumps a gram of the white powder down the drain, throwing the dollar bill I had rolled and a plastic business card all into the garbage disposal. Next, he stomps the small wooden box on the floor and smashes it into tiny pieces, tossing it into the disposal as well. "Do you have anything else here or anywhere else?" he asks after shutting off the noisy machine.

"That's all there is," I snap, pushing past him to open the fridge. While trying to control my anger, I grab a bottle of water and down it. I'm angry at myself, at the embarrassment I feel due to this weakness.

"Do you have a duffle or something to put some stuff in?"

David walks down the hall to the bedroom, completely ignoring my outburst.

"There should be one in the closet." I walk toward the bedroom. I open up the dresser and grab the few clothes out of the drawers, tossing them into the bag.

David empties the closet in no time, keeping the clothes hanging on the hangers. "Anything else?"

I go to the back of the closet and move aside a loose piece of paneling to reveal a shelf that holds my badge and extra ammunition along with my side arm. "That's it," I tell him.

As we walk out of the tiny dull apartment toward David's truck, I have no emotions of loss or hope. I'm emotionally empty. How can a person not feel anything about… well anything?

Is this what my life has become since meth? Meaningless, void of existence? I always thought I was doing meth to forget my guilt and emotions, who knew quitting was the best way to go numb.

My phone chimes in my pocket, dragging me out of the dark thoughts that have taken over my mind.

Checking on you. I could tell you weren't overjoyed with the idea of staying with Macy and David. If it gets to be too much, just be honest with them. I'm always here. Later, Rosie

I get in the truck and glance back at the dark apartment; I turn to David. "Thanks for coming with me. If I had come alone or stayed here, I would have used the drugs that were in there. I thought I could handle it on my own, but clearly I can't."

"Hey, man, this isn't going to be something you can kick

overnight. One day at a time. Macy, Rosie, and I are here to help you anyway we can. Can I ask when you started to use?"

I get uncomfortably silent and look out the window as I rub my sweaty palms down the thigh of my jeans to dry them off, stalling to come up with a suitable answer to David's question. "When undercover, once in a while I couldn't find a way out of it, but the night Macy was shot was the first time I went looking for it. I bought it."

"Fuck, Mike… I blamed you at the hospital, I had no right to do that. It wasn't your fault what happened to Macy."

"Logically, I know. Something just clicked in my brain when I saw Macy drop. Shooting Jack didn't fix it. Then seeing her laying in the hospital bed pushed me over the edge."

We pull into the drive back at the house, and I begin to shake. It started with my hands, now my entire body. David pulls into the drive and calls Rosie.

He has the phone on speaker as I hear him tell her what is going on.

She replies, "Get him in the house and give him some juice. Let him lie down. Unfortunately, he's going to go through this for a while. Mike, do you want me to come over?"

"No," I respond, opening my door and getting out of the car. I stumble a few steps before regaining my footing as Macy walks out the door.

She stops, not saying anything.

I kiss her on the forehead. "I'm going to go lie down," I tell her and continue into the house.

I don't even bother turning on the light or kicking off my shoes. I flop on my bed and curl into the fetal position. I'm exhausted, feeling as if I haven't slept in days; I pull the blanket over me and sleep.

* * *

I wake with a start.

Sitting up in the dark room, I wonder where I am and scoot up to where my back is against the headboard; my arm bumps something on the table next to me. I reach over to catch it and realize it's a lamp. Turning it on, I have to shield my eyes from the sudden brightness that invades the room. When my eyes adjust, I glance around and quickly realize I'm in my childhood bedroom.

Thinking I have been asleep for hours, I look at the time on my phone: ten in the evening. I've only been down for an hour. I decide to go find my stuff. I quietly open the door and step out into the dark hall, making my way into the living room.

David and Macy must have gone to bed; the television is off, and the house is quiet. I turn and walk into the kitchen when I see something out of the corner of my eye. I can only slightly make out the silhouette of a man.

I move to the other side of the cabinets and get a knife from the stand on the counter. Crouching down, I crawl along the floor, so I'm not detected by the intruder. I jump to my feet, jerking the door to the laundry room open and yell, "Freeze, police!"

The kitchen light comes on, and I'm momentarily blinded by the light. "Mike, what the fuck are you doing?" Macy asks. "Why do you have a knife in your hand?"

David comes running into the kitchen with a towel around his waist and water dripping from his body. "What's going on?"

"Mike was going to stab the dryer," Macy says dryly, walking up and removing the knife out of my hand, then replacing it where it belongs. "Let's go back to bed, Mike. Everything is all right." She places her head on my shoulder, taking my hand in hers. "David, baby, can you get the lights?" she asks as we walk down the hall.

"I'm sorry, Macy." I'm ashamed of all the stupid stuff I keep pulling.

"I'm not sure what's going on with me."

"Little brother, it's time to be honest with yourself. You're detoxing. The next few weeks are going to be an up and down battle." Macy climbs on to the bed with her back against the headboard.

I join her. "How do you know so much about this?"

"I did a lot of research so I could help Rosie. The first few days you can experience: anxiety, depression, exhaustion, hallucination, panic, paranoia, sleepiness, and suicidal thoughts. This is why we wanted you here with us so we can help you."

"I don't understand why you would want to help me. I didn't do anything to help you or Marcus. Now he's dead, and you were almost killed."

"Wow, David was right, you really do have a god complex, don't you?"

I sit up straight, my fist double at my side. "What the fuck does that mean?"

"What I mean, little brother, is I didn't know you were

some kind of superhero and shit. When Marcus went to work for Jack, you were what, fourteen or fifteen? I went to work for Jack after Marcus was killed to keep you from going. I wasn't going to lose another brother to him. We both know how that worked out: you became a cop that we could all be proud of and saved me from Jack." She turns my head so I'm looking at her. "Mike, you saved me. You brought me back to David, alive. You killed Jack; I never have to live in fear again. You did that, Mike. *You* saved me."

"I did all that?" I look at her with eyes filled with tears.

"You did all that, for me and for David."

I'm suddenly so tired; I feel as if the weight of the world has been lifted off my chest. I curl up next to Macy, holding her hand, and go to sleep.

I must have gone into a deep sleep. I don't wake until there is a knock on my door. "Come in."

"Hey, you still up for going to the gym with me this morning?" David asks, standing in the doorway.

"I am. Do I have time for some coffee and to change?"

"Sure, see you in the kitchen."

When I walk into the kitchen, I see Macy sitting on David's lap at the table. "Sorry, I didn't mean to interrupt," I tell them, going to the cabinet and getting a cup for coffee.

"You didn't interrupt," Macy replies. "How do you feel after getting some sleep?"

"I'm good this morning. Maybe sleep is what I needed to get back on my feet." I take a seat at the table, feeling good about myself today. I had my detox last night. My hallucination in the kitchen, then the exhaustion afterward. I went to sleep and woke up feeling like my old self again. I kept telling everyone I didn't have the addiction they all seemed to think I had.

I'll work out with David today, go to the meeting with Rosie this afternoon, and swing by the department to let the Chief know I'm ready to return to work.

"Ready to go?" David asks, patting me on the shoulder.

"Of course." I jump up eager to get the day started. I give Macy a kiss on the cheek and tell her, "Have a great day."

CHAPTER TWO

ROSIE

I'm getting my first cup of coffee when my phone rings. I know instantly who it is by the *"You Are My Sunshine"* ringtone. "Morning, Macy." I groan into the phone. Macy's morning mood makes me want to beat her to a bloody pulp. Too damn happy in the morning, even before coffee. Since her and David got married, it's gotten worse.

I'm kidding. I love Macy and David. Macy is my sister for life. She has been there when no others were. She pushed me to pursue my talent, gave me a job, and trusted me to manage her tattoo shop for her.

"Hi, Doll! Want to meet at the diner and get some breakfast before we go work out?"

"Macy… What happened last night? You never want to go work out this early. Mike told me he was going to the gym with David."

"Nothing," she replies, the truth shining through that one word. Something's up and Macy needs to talk.

"I'll pick up breakfast and be there in a few. Put some coffee on."

"Thanks, Rosie."

I throw on my hoodie and tennis shoes, as I call the diner around the corner from Macy's house to order our normal breakfast for mornings that we're going to have seriously long talks: tall stack of chocolate chip pancakes, extra bacon, and warm maple syrup. I walk out the diner with what looks like enough food for four people.

When I pull up to the house, the door opens, and Macy greets me with a smile and hug. "Thank gawd we don't eat like this very often or we would both weigh a thousand pounds."

She laughs, taking two of the bags out of my hands.

Putting the bags on the coffee table, I see Macy has everything set for our talk. The couch has pillows, a couple of blankets, Kleenex on the coffee table, and the TV is ready to play Pretty Woman if needed.

"This is serious, otherwise we'd be watching Thelma and Louise and planning our escape," I joke with her.

"David and I are great." She flops down on the couch, pulling a pillow into her lap and hugging it securely.

"I know, sweetie." I gently squeeze her knee as I sit down. "You're having a rough time seeing Mike deal with his addiction, aren't you?"

"No, it's not really that. The fact that he's not dealing with it bothers me more."

"I'm not following you." I lean back, pulling my feet up under me.

"Mike was hallucinating last night, thinking there was someone in the kitchen. He had a knife. When he realized it was just me, he went to bed, curled up next to me, and slept all night. When he woke up, it was as if he was cured. Ready to go to the gym and to go talk to the Chief about going back to work."

"Oh."

"Oh? That's all you have to say?"

"Macy, come on. You remember what it's like. I know he's your baby brother and all, but you of all people should know he's going to have to go through this his own way." I'm instantly struck with guilt for all the shit I put my friend through as she stood beside me, dragging me to meetings, making me face my demons, and dealing with the crap I never wanted to touch, let alone face.

Now I sit here and scold her for being upset for watching her brother go through the same thing. I'm a terrible friend, childish, jealous, and immature after everything Macy has done for me.

"Fuck, I really am a bitch, aren't I?" I admit, scooting over next to Macy and taking her hands into mine.

"Yeah, you really are," Macy answers, wiping her eyes. "But I love you, anyway."

"I love you too." I make her a plate of food and hand it to her, then make myself one. We eat and watch the movie. Before we know it, we have devoured the entire breakfast.

Both of us are sound asleep when Macy's phone rings, waking us. "Hello?" she groggily answers.

A smile creeps across her face, letting me know it's David on the other end of the call. I sit up and clear away the evidence of carbohydrate indulgence. I gather our plates and head into the kitchen. I had just finished loading the dishwasher when Macy comes into the room.

"David called to see if we would meet them at the diner for breakfast before your meeting," Macy announces with a sly look on her face.

"You told him we just ate enough food for five people, right?" I toss the dish towel at her and lean against the counter. "Macy, you told him, right?"

"I couldn't, Rosie. It's so sweet that he wants us to come eat with them."

"It's not going to be cute when we puke pancakes all over the diner," I counter.

"Come on, Rosie, we can do this." Macy begins to get ready.

I pretend to grumble as I get ready, but I can't help but smile at Macy's happiness. The two of them have gone through ten years of hell to be together. I will endure whatever to help her out, even if I gain twenty pounds in the process. "It's a good thing David owns a gym," I tell her as I button my jeans. "I'm going to have to hire him as a trainer if we don't give up pancakes soon."

Macy laughs as she ties her shoes and grimaces when she stands back up. "Maybe he'll give us a group rate?"

"Did he say anything about how Mike did this morning?" I ask as we walk out to my car and get in.

"No, I figured Mike was right there, so I didn't ask. We'll see soon enough."

"Don't worry, I'll help him the way you did me. You just have to remember this is his journey, not yours." I reach over, giving her hand a squeeze before pulling into a parking spot next to David's car.

We walk into the diner and see David and Mike in a booth toward the back. They both get up when we walk up to let us slide in. Mike and I face the door.

A huge stake of pancakes sits in the middle of the table.

Mike and David both bust out laughing, looking at Macy and me. "I told you, David. I knew they pigged out already." Mike laughed while looking at us.

I elbow Mike in the rib. "How did you know?"

"I remember you two would always get together to talk about stuff and eat pancakes watching chick flicks," Mike said proudly. "You should have seen your faces. You both were green when you saw the pancakes." He laughs again.

"Macy, why didn't you tell me you ate when I called?" David asked her.

She looks at me for help. "Oh, come on, David. No female wants to admit we downed enough pancakes for four people… especially to someone that owns a gym and is built like you and Buns of Steel."

"Buns of Steel?" Mike turns in the seat to look at me. "So, you been checking out my ass, have you Rosie?"

I'm cornered in the booth seat with nowhere to go. "Maybe." I shrug my shoulders. "It's not like I can check him out anymore." I nod my head toward David. "He ruined it by marrying my best friend. I guess that leaves you, even though you are a cop." I grin at him.

"What's wrong with cops?" he asks before taking a drink of his coffee.

"You're too law abiding." I wrinkle my nose at him. "But… you do come with your own set of handcuffs." I wink at him.

"Okay, Rosie… enough. He's my brother, and I'm sitting right here," Macy contests, pretending to put her hands over her ears to block out what I'm saying.

Everyone laughs, except Mike. "Rosie, get your cell phone out and dial 911. Let me know when they pick up." Mike's face is deadly serious as he watches some guys come into the diner.

"What's going on?" Everyone asks at the same time.

"They are on the phone, Mike."

"Tell them there are two men with guns at the diner, approximately twenty people inside and six staff. One person is an off-duty undercover officer without a weapon. Then put your phone in your pocket but don't hang up."

I lean over and whisper to Mike, putting my hand on my hand on his strong muscular thigh. "They said they are sending officers."

CHAPTER THREE

MIKE

My adrenaline kicks in as I realize I'm unarmed, and my family is in harm's way. "David, I want you to take both girls and walk out of the diner. I'll stop at the register to pay."

"No way, you don't have a gun. The girls will leave. I'll wait by the door to give you back up."

"Okay. Macy, Rosie, straight out the door and to the car. Go to the end of the block while staying on the phone with the station."

"Please be careful," Macy says.

When we get up by the two-armed men, I give Rosie a hug as David kisses Macy. "Talk to you later, ladies." I walk up to the register.

No sooner has the door closed then the two men pull out their guns and tell everyone to hand over their cell phones and wallets. Both men have turned their attention on David since he is much larger than they are. He's not as accommodating as the other patrons of the diner are at handing over his wallet.

I quietly walked up behind the closest gunman, tapping him on the shoulder. As he spins around, I grab his wrist, holding the gun with my left hand, and punch him with my right fist, causing his head to thrust backward. At the same time, David uppercuts the second man and tackles him to the ground.

By the time the police arrive, we have the guns away from both men and have them sitting on the steps out front with their hands zip tied, courtesy of the diner owner.

Rosie and Macy had come back to us when they saw us come out. I got on the phone and explained to the Desk Sergeant what had happened. He then connected me to my Sergeant who informed me not to move until he was on scene.

"Detective Anderson, you are supposed to be off duty, would you like to explain to me why you are apprehending two armed robbers?" a deep booming voice behind me asks.

"Sir, I was having breakfast with my family when the perps walked in. I observed what was going on and had Rosie call it in. We got my sister and Rosie outside the diner and were able to disarm the two men without any issue, and that's how it happened."

"Do you realize you allowed a civilian to aid you? You not only put him in harm's way but everyone in the diner as well."

"Sir, I'm not sure you are aware who the civilian is."

"I don't give a rat's ass who he is. You don't allow citizens to do police work," he yelled.

"I wasn't in any danger," David tells him.

"David Martin, what are you doing here?" my Sergeant asks him.

"Mike is my brother-in-law. We were having breakfast with my wife, his sister, and her friend. I wasn't in danger. The man didn't have his gun pulled. If a boxer can't handle a common neighborhood punk, then I need to hang up my gloves, don't you think?" David winks at the man.

"As long as he hadn't brandished his firearm at the time, I guess we can let that slide." The Sergeant shakes David's hand, before turning back to me. "How are you doing?"

"I'm doing good, worked out at the gym this morning. I have a sponsor." I pointed at Rosie. "We are headed to another meeting. I can handle coming back to work, Sir."

He doesn't respond to me as he turns. "David, I've heard great things about your after school program at the gym. How many kids have you got now?" Sarge asks David.

"We have fifteen with a waiting list because we don't have enough volunteers," David responds.

"Anderson, come by the station tomorrow around noon, so we can talk."

"Yes, Sir," I tell him.

David pats me on the back. "That sounds promising," David says to me as we walk toward Macy and Rosie.

"Are you ready to go to our meeting?" I ask Rosie.

"Yes. Macy, do you need a ride home?"

"I'll drive her," David says. "Mike, I'll see you back at the gym later on."

I wave at him and Macy as I climb into Rosie's truck with her.

"Admit it, my truck is growing on you, isn't it?" she asks as we pull out into traffic.

"It's a pretty decent ride."

"Why did you choose a Harley instead of something more practical in the wintertime?"

"I have a pickup. The bike works best with my job. It's easy to change parts on so it's not recognizable, but I still have something of mine with me that I know runs good."

"Where is your truck?"

"I keep it at the station. That way it's out of view of most people. I can get it at a moment's notice if needed."

"Sounds like a confusing way to live your life." Rosie pulls into the parking lot of the building where the N.A. meetings are held. "I understand why it would be easy to get lost in such a confusing world. You never know when one world ends and one begins."

I never thought of it like that, I think to myself as we get out and head inside. Today's meeting has a lot more people in it. I decide not to share and neither does Rosie. We both seem lost in the events of this morning.

After the meeting is over, we are back in the truck. "What are you thinking about?" I ask Rosie.

She continues to drive without answering until we pull up outside the gym. Shutting off the truck she turns to face me. "We really aren't that different, Mike. No matter what you think. I turned to drugs because I didn't think I was worthy of having a family to care for me. You turned to drugs because you didn't think you were worthy, either... because you couldn't protect your family." She reaches over and takes my hand in hers. "The really sad thing is we both love the same family and did the same stupid shit to get their attention."

"For some unknown reason, they love us unconditionally."

"Yep, they are the idiots, not us," Rosie says and starts laughing.

I can't help but join in.

After a few minutes, David walks out of the gym and stands at the side of the truck to stare at us with his massive arms crossed over his chest. "What the fuck is wrong with the two of you? Clients are coming in complaining there are a couple of drunks out here."

That starts Rosie and I off on another laughing fit. We both have tears running down our cheeks as David stands there staring at us like we have lost our minds.

Finally able to catch my breath, I get out of the truck. "Thanks for the ride. I'll talk to you later, Rosie." I put an arm on David's shoulder, turning him around to go back in the gym. "Man, you need to loosen up. You're really tense today. Have you thought about laughing? It does wonders for tension." I turn and give one last wave to Rosie.

Once inside, David puts me to work with a new client and showing him how the machines work and the correct form to use on each one. This isn't what I want to do with my days, but it sure beats sitting around staring at the walls.

I can do what needs to be done around here to help them out and at the house. I make my mind up to not wallow in self-pity but to be an asset to help my family any way I can.

Pops is David's partner in the gym. He comes by to let me know David went to pick up the kids. This is going to be my first time working with them.

Pops started the program as a way to keep David and my brother Marcus from joining the Guardians. A gang ran by David's father and brother, Jack. They eventually started to force kids from the local schools to join or face the consequences.

Since taking down the Guardians, the parents are more eager than ever to have their kids enrolled in a worthwhile after school program that keeps them safe and teaches them self-defense.

Within ten minutes, David is back with the teens. The volume in the gym goes up to a ten.

Pops comes out of his office and lets out a shrill whistle. "Who has homework?"

All seven boys raise their hands while the eight females shake their heads.

"Why am I not surprised?" Pops shakes his head. "Into the office, men."

The boys grab their gear and grumble as they walk off to finish what they didn't get done at school.

"Okay, ladies. Since you have your stuff done and are ready to go today, I'll go ahead and introduce you to Mike Anderson, my brother-in-law. He is going to be helping me out around here for a while."

"I'll be in the ring working on sparring while Mike will keep an eye on you at the machines. Any questions?"

David takes half the females to warm up in the ring, while I take the other half to the punching bags. To my surprise, once the training starts, the girls' chit chat goes quiet. After the guys finished their schoolwork, they change and join the warm up.

David and Pops have two groups sparring at a time. I have never witnessed kids being so supportive of each other and encouraging.

This is what David is meant to do with his life. You can see the pride filling him as each kid succeeds at trying something new. I have never seen a man enjoy his life the way David does.

That is how I want to live my life. One small victory at a time, helping others along the way. I don't want to live in a constant state of fear, that someone I care about is going to die, because I'm not good enough to protect them.

My phone rings and I go into the office to answer it when I see that it's the Chief. "Yes, sir. I'm on my way," I respond to the man's command. Walking out of the office, I get David's attention and motion for him to come toward me.

"I got a call and have to go to the station. I'll be back to catch up with you later."

"Do you need to take my car? Pops can drop me at the house later."

"If you don't mind, that way I can pick up my bike. Thanks."

I go to the office, get the key, and head out. My mind races, wondering what is so important that the Chief is calling me in right away.

Pulling up to the house, I run inside. "Macy, you home?" I call out. I see a note on the fridge.

Have a portrait at the shop. Swing by and we can grab tacos for dinner. Love you both, M.

Now I feel like a shit for taking David's car. When I get

done at the station, I can go back and pick him up. It feels good to climb onto my Harley with my head clear.

I enter the station; I no longer have the strut of confidence of a seasoned undercover detective. I look ahead and not at any other officers; afraid I will see the betrayal in their eyes. I had let them down by being weak. No longer do I have their backs if they need me.

I knock on the Chief's door, instantly hearing enter. When I open the door, I'm told to have a seat. He picks up the phone to tell someone I had arrived.

A moment later, the door opens and in walks the Sargent. "Anderson, I wasn't expecting to see you till tomorrow."

I stand to shake his hand. "Yes, sir."

"Have a seat. The reason we called you in is because Butcher Maxon has gotten out of prison."

I'm instantly on my feet. "What do you mean Butcher is out of prison? How the fuck did that happen?"

"There was some kind of mess up with the paperwork, and he was released instead of another prisoner."

"That wasn't a mix up. That was planned. Do we know where he is headed? Has he made it back to Oklahoma City yet?"

"That's where you come in. Do you think you can handle yourself enough to go back undercover with the Disciples? I know it's a lot to ask of you, but I don't have anyone else." He pats me on the shoulder. "We have to get him back inside before the bodies start to fall."

"I need a new place to crash." I'll go downstairs and pick up a new burner phone and other equipment. "I'm going to go let my family know I'm back to work. Then I'll be in touch."

"Mike, watch your ass. Don't miss a check-in."

"I know." I exit the office.

The familiar surge of adrenaline courses through my veins as I go down to the basement to get supplies: a cell phone with a tracer that cannot be detected, several listening devices, small cameras for surveillance, ammo, and a couple of extra guns. The officer behind the counter hands me my new identification. Well, it's really not new. It's the same persona I've been going by for the last year and half, while being undercover within the Disciples, as Mikey Andrews.

My phone dings, giving me the address of the new place I will be calling home for a while. I swing by and stash my gear. I give David a call and ask him if he can meet me at the tattoo shop at six.

I grab tacos from the truck at the end of the block from the tattoo shop for everyone for dinner. I'm aware my news isn't going to be received very well; I hope Macy understands why I have to do it.

I meet David in the parking lot. "Mike what's up? Why are you dressed like that?"

I'm dressed in leathers, my bike boots, and the fenders on my Harley have been switched out to where the chrome is gone; my bike looks worn and less custom.

"Mike, are you going back under?"

"I have to. One of the Disciples escaped prison."

"Are you sure you can handle it?" David asks, leaning against his car. "Macy is going to be heart broken."

"Why do you think I asked you to meet me here? I'm not

afraid to face the Disciples, but I'm terrified to face her alone," I joke.

"I never said you were dumb."

"Let's go get this over with. I'm hoping I can get one more meeting in before I go tonight." We enter the tattoo shop as Macy finishes up with her client and cleans her station. Rosie is letting him out the front door and locking it as I announce, "I brought tacos."

"A man that knows his way to my heart." Rosie laughs as she takes the tacos from me and walks toward the office. "How are you doing tonight?"

"I'm good, Rosie." I follow her, leaving David and Macy in the other room. "Rosie, I was wondering if you would be up to going to a meeting with me tonight?"

"Of course, are you doing all right?"

"I'm good." Macy and David walk in.

Everyone is quiet as they begin to eat. When we are done, Rosie says, "I'm ready to go to the meeting."

"We still have a few minutes. I need to talk to you all about something important. I was called back to the station today. I have to report back to work."

"Wait, you what? You're not ready to go back to work yet?" Rosie is the first one to react.

Macy doesn't say anything. She just sits there and holds David's hand in hers, tears rolling down her cheeks. "Macy, aren't you going to say anything?"

"What do you want me to say? You're a grown-ass man. This is your job, your life. You don't need your older sister stepping in telling you what to do."

I stand to get ready to go, and so does everyone else.

Macy doesn't say anything else to me until she grabs me and gives me a hug. "Don't get dead."

"I love you, sis. I'll be back soon." I hold my pinky finger up to her.

She holds her pinky finger up before wrapping it in mine. "I'll never forgive you if you die."

"I know, I'm more afraid of you then the guys I'm hunting."

"You should be." She pulls me into a hug. "I love you, Mike."

"Rosie, you're not saying anything," Macy says after she releases me.

"What am I supposed to say? This is a family matter." Rosie grabs her jacket and puts it on. "Ready for the meeting?"

"Yes, I'll follow you there," Rosie's answer is like a kick in the gut.

"No, you finish your goodbyes. I'll see you there." She gives Macy a quick hug. "See you tomorrow." Without another word, Rosie is out the backdoor and gone.

I look at Macy and David confused as to what just happened.

"She's worried about you, Mike." Macy tells me.

"I'll try to talk to her some more after the meeting." I give Macy another quick hug. "See you both soon."

I leave the shop, climb on my bike, and head to the community center where tonight's meeting is being held. As I park, I look around the lot and don't see that many people in attendance for this evening's meeting.

Maybe fifteen people ventured out tonight, only a couple

of people I recognize from other meetings; Rosie is talking to a young couple. She hasn't noticed me.

It's a nice meeting, but I don't share. Rosie sits next to me. I reach over a take her hand into mine. "Are you all, right?"

"Of course," she responds quickly without looking at me.

They call an end to the meeting. I stand, keeping a hold of Rosie's hand, and pull her toward the door.

"What are you doing? Let go of me." She tries to jerk free of my grasp. A few of the meeting attendees heard her as we walk past them to the door.

I stop turning to face her. My mouth next to her ear so she can clearly hear me. "We are going outside and you're going to tell me what the fuck is wrong."

Rosie pulls free and walks out the door, letting it freely fly back at me as I walk outside behind her. To my relief, she doesn't walk toward her truck but toward the alley. "You're going to use again." She wastes no time spitting her judgement at me.

"Don't you think I'm worried about that?" I run my hand through my hair, frustrated. "I won't be able to pick up the phone and call you if I need to talk." I lean against the building beside her. "It takes years to get where I am in this investigation. The guy I'm after will hurt a lot of people if I don't stop him."

"Be careful." She grabs the front of my shirt in her fist.

"I will be. You will be the first call I make when I'm done." Her grip on my shirt loosens. "Are you going to pick up when I call?"

"Maybe." She smiles, stands on her tiptoes, and gives me a

quick kiss. "I've been waiting a year for you to call me, or have you forgotten?"

"Rosie, I have never stopped thinking about that night. Let me get this mess cleaned up so we can talk. What do you say?" I lean in to kiss her when I see a man around six feet tall, slim build, in a black leather jacket, and jeans. His long, shaggy, dirty blond hair catches my attention from across the street. I whisper to her, "Rosie, pretend you don't know me. Head to your truck now. Don't look back."

Rosie does what I say, she is in her truck as I walk out of the dark alley. I look to make sure there are no cars as I jog across the road toward the man. "Duke? Man, is that you?" Duke is a wanna-be that hangs around the Disciples and gets them what they need. He is nothing more than a gopher for the gang.

He stops, his hand instantly going to his pocket. He's armed. "Who the fuck? Wait… Mikey?"

"Yeah, man, it's me."

"You look different."

"The heat was after me when I was on the West Coast, so I had to bounce, cut off my hair, lost the beard." I look around as if I'm making sure we aren't being followed.

"When did you get back in town?" Duke asks, following my lead and looking around.

"About thirty minutes ago," I reply. "Anything happening around here? I need to make some money?"

"Give me a call tomorrow. I'll see what I can find out."

"I'd appreciate it." I wave and jog across the street, making it seem as if I'm heading in the opposite direction of Duke.

When I'm sure Duke is out of the area, I circle back and get my bike.

I arrive at the new safe house that I'll be using as my place while I'm under. I walk in and flip on the lights. The room floods with a yellow glow, illuminating the white walls and tan carpet in the living room. The place is sparsely furnished with furniture at least twenty years old.

I open the fridge. They went shopping and filled it when they prepped the apartment. Going into the bedroom, I reach my hand behind the headboard. To my relief, my two guns and my knife I've always carried in my boot are fastened behind the headboard. Under the mattress, I find cameras and listening devices together with more information to build our case.

My cell phone buzzes, alerting me it's time to do my first check-in with my handler at the station. I dial the number; when it's picked up, I quickly say, "Detective, badge number 3517. First check-in, made contact."

Usually, I get a ten-four and the next time I'm supposed to check-in, but I'm told to hold for further instructions.

"Anderson, Butcher has grabbed one of the jurors that sat on his trial. He took him right in front of his family. I'm sending a picture of the man to your phone. He was the jury foreman."

"Where?"

"The man and his family had been out to dinner. They were going to the car after leaving the restaurant on Thomas Street. Butcher pulled a gun and took James Douglas with him."

"We have no idea where he would have taken him?" I ask, looking through the information on my phone.

"No, he's had him three hours already. Who did you make contact with?"

"I ran into Duke. He thinks I just got back into town from the West Coast. I told him I was looking for work."

"Good . Don't waste your time on small scale jobs. We need to find Butcher."

"Yes, Sir." I hang up the phone, then pop a pot pie in the microwave. I get myself back into character by going over my notes and to see if there are any clues I may have forgotten.

Two hours later, I have gone over everything and everyone. Nothing jumps out at me. I decide to call it a night and get some sleep.

CHAPTER FOUR

MIKE

James Douglas was found in pieces on the steps of the courthouse in Oklahoma City, every part of him accounted for except for his head.

Thank goodness he was discovered by the security guards before court was due to open this morning or the entire courthouse area would have been flooded with people on their way to work and evidence destroyed.

My first stop is the coroner's office. I walk into the basement and through the plastic curtain that covers the door to the morgue drop-off.

"Sally, you in here?" I call out, so I don't startle her. Sally has been the State Coroner for the last ten years. She is someone I trust completely.

"I'm here," she yells back to me. As I enter the examination room, she looks up at me. "What the hell are you doing back so soon? You promised me you were going to take some time and get your head on straight."

"That's exactly what I was doing until this shit started." I point to the human jigsaw puzzle on her table.

"What did he use to chop him up? A chainsaw?" I put on gloves and lift the right forearm. The skin and meat aren't cut straight through. The blade looks as if it chewed through the flesh. The radius and ulna are cut clean and straight through. "Any idea what kind of saw would do this?" I ask.

"If I didn't know the Butcher was locked up in McAllister, I would swear this was his handiwork with a reciprocating saw."

"That's why I'm back Sandy, he escaped. This poor bastard was the jury foreman at the Butcher's trial."

"Shit, that means there are at least eleven other possible victims out there." She shakes her head and gets back to work. "Are you sure you're okay to be back so soon?"

"I'm going to do my best to keep it together. Thanks for looking out for me. I got to head out. Talk to you later."

"Stay safe, Mike."

CHAPTER FIVE

ROSIE

I can't believe Mike thinks he is all right to go back to work. Doesn't he realize five meetings doesn't cure anyone? That's not how NA works.

I wonder if he was really called back to work or if he was just chasing everyone away so he could go back to using. Maybe I should let Macy know my theory. I know she would go out and look for him on the streets with me, though.

What if he really is back undercover and I do something stupid and blow his cover and he gets hurt? Macy would never forgive me. I would never forgive myself. I'm rambling like a mad woman. Why am I so concerned with what he is doing or where he is at?

I'm not, I decide. I grab my gym bag and head out the door toward my truck.

Macy walks out of the gym. "Hey, girl. Thanks for meeting

me here today. I can't keep doing the pancake breakfasts." She gives me a hug. "Are you all, right?"

"Yeah, I'm good. I didn't sleep well last night."

"Did a certain cop leaving have anything to do with that?" She pushes me with her hand as we walk inside.

"What are trying to say?"

"It's okay if you're into Mike. I would love it if the two of you got together, Rosie."

"Whoa... Macy, you need to tap the breaks." I put my bag into a locker. "I was going to be his sponsor." I let her start to wrap my hands. "I have no desire to start anything with him or anyone else."

"My bad. I thought I saw some sparks between the two of you. I'll drop it."

"Thank you, now can we work out please?"

We spend the next hour working out, neither of us saying much to the other. We stop by the office to say goodbye to Pops and David before going to Macy's to take showers before heading to the tattoo shop.

As we walk into the office, there is breaking news flashing on the television. A Channel Three newscaster appears on the TV.

"We have a positive identification to the body that was found on the steps to the courthouse this morning. The person has been identified as the jury foreman James Douglas in the Butcher Maxon trial.

We have no details as to how Butcher Maxon was able to escape the maximum-security McAllister Prison. The Chief of Police and the Warden are to hold a press conference later this week.

We have just been informed by Chief Lovel that juror number ten, K.D. Baker's husband, has just filed a missing person report on him after

Baker did not come home from his job at Beef Cakes, where he is the main attraction.

"Wow, Rosie, you've done work on that guy."

"I've even seen his act. He is a killer Cher impersonator." I lean against desk when I realize why Mike was called back to work.

"Young lady, you're pretty pale. Are you feeling all right?" Pops reaches down and gets a bottle of water out of the mini fridge. "Drink this."

"I'm good. It was a shock seeing someone I know missing on the news is all." I drink some water and catch David watching me.

He shakes his head. I give him a quick understanding nod; he has come to the same conclusion I have about Mike's sudden call back to work. "Macy, we should get going. We need to be there when the deliveries arrive at the shop."

"You're right. Have a good day, Pops. Talk to you later."

"You two try to stay out of trouble." He waves and goes back to work.

"David, can you walk Rosie and I to the car?" Macy asks, giving him a pouty look.

"Sure." He takes Macy's hand, and we walk outside to the parking lot. "I'll check with you later this afternoon to see how your day's going." He leans down to kiss Macy.

Macy says, "I hope you don't seriously think you are the only two that figured out Mike went back to work to track the Butcher? I can't believe you both thought I wouldn't figure it out. I know what cases Mike used to work. He would always check in with me when he could."

"Macy, we were just trying to protect you," David tells her.

"I get that, I really do, but what I need is honesty, trust, and for you two to be there for me no matter what without any secrets."

"You're right, Macy, I'm sorry." I give her a hug.

"The only thing we can do is trust that Mike can handle it. He will catch this sick bastard and come home, safe and sound." She gives David a kiss. "We have to get to the shop. I love you."

"Love you. By Rosie," David waves.

CHAPTER SIX

MIKE

K.D.'s husband is coming into the station and agrees to meet with me today. Don Baker is the owner of Beefcakes where K.D. works. I do not enter the interview room. Instead, I go into the connecting room next to it while I observe Don's reaction as my Chief questions him.

He paces, wringing his hands. Don looks more worried than he does guilty or frightened. Chief Lovel enters the room, preparing to get some answers.

"Mr. Baker, I'm Chief Lovel. We appreciate you coming in to talk with me under such trying times. Can you tell me about the evening leading up to K.D.'s disappearance?"

"K.D. came to work as he always does. Everyone loved him. He's always in a good mood. The staff loved him as much as the customers did. K.D. had a way about him that put everyone at ease." His eyes lit up as he described his husband. When he had stopped talking, his face was filled with pain and fear.

"Had K.D. been approached by anyone since the trial was over?" Chief asks.

"No, K.D. didn't talk about being on the jury. That was something he took very seriously. Everyone thinks being on a jury is a pain in the ass, not K.D." He takes a drink of the bottle of water a deputy had brought him. "He wanted to be on that jury."

"Why?"

"That's the case of a lifetime. People become overnight sensations after something like that. He knew the publicity for that kind of case would be wild."

"Did K.D. understand, going into that jury, what the dangers of a case like that could have?" he asks.

After all these years, I'm still amazed what people will do for the fifteen minutes of fame. Do they not understand the responsibility that comes with being a juror?

"K.D. said the Judge told them they would be safe. He kept telling me not to worry. Once the man was in jail, there would be no chance he'd get out." The emotions became too much for him, as he began to shake, and his breathing became haggard.

"Take deep breaths, Don. Slow your breathing down." Chief Lovel pulls his chair back from the table and turns Don to face him. "We are doing everything we can to bring K.D. home to you."

After taking a break, Don was asked if he had any security footage from the club of the last night K.D. was there. If he is really the diva Don made him sound like, he would want to have his shows recorded so he could rewatch them.

"Of course, K.D. recorded everything."

"I would like to send one of our officers over to pick up the footage."

"I can call and have them have it ready for you," Don offers.

"I would appreciate that. The officer will take you home on his way to get it. I assure you, we will keep you updated with any news we have."

I take a moment to call Duke after sending Don off.

"Yeah?" is all he says when he answers the phone.

"Duke, man, it's Mikey."

"Yo, dude. I was wondering if I was going to hear from you. I have some work right up your alley."

"What is it?"

"I'm not discussing it on the phone. Meet me in thirty minutes at Tenth and Maple."

"Sure, but Duke, I'm not looking for some small-time action, man, so don't be wasting my time," I push.

"Mikey, I got you. See you in a few minutes." The phone goes dead.

I go downstairs and have them ensure the tracker on my phone and the one in my boot is working, in case this turns into a set up. I wear what looks like a handmade metal cross around my neck. I've always told everyone my old man made it, that's why I never take it off. Really, it's a camera.

For me, each character when I'm undercover has specific things unique to them. This helps me stay in character and keep them separate. Plus, it's always been an easy way to hide any electronics I need to have on me.

We do a quick rundown of the equipment before I head to the meeting site. I arrive right on time to Duke leaning against the building, waiting on me.

"Right on time. I've always liked that about you, Mikey." His grin shows a mouth full of broken, sharp, rotten teeth from years of drug use.

When he's talking, I look away to avoid the stench of his breath. "We only have to go down here." He nods his head down the dark alley behind him.

I quietly follow him, putting my hand in my pocket around the knife, just in case I need it. We walk until the alley dead ends. There is an abandoned warehouse on the right and an old dress shop to the left, headless mannequins still stand in the window partially dressed in the latest fashions from years ago.

Duke walks up to the warehouse, rapidly knocking on the door three times. I stand there looking all around, making sure we aren't about to be ambushed.

The door slowly begins to open. I realize this is the new Disciples Club house. Visitors to the club turn over weapons. I turned in my two pistols and the knife I had in my pocket. I'd get them back when I left as long as I was allowed to leave. I always kept a pistol in one boot and a knife in the other that are never turned over to anyone.

I'm welcomed back into the club with pats on the back and chest pulled in for an embrace. When in reality, they were patting me down to make sure I'm still trustworthy.

There are some clubs out there that I completely respect. Disciples are not one of them. They are a dangerous, deadly group that seeks revenge on anyone that has done them wrong, or anyone that has something they want.

Tonight's female entertainment walks into the room. Over half of them barely look sixteen. I try to face them so my camera can get a good look at their faces. A flash of red hair catches my attention, causing my dick to go hard. I make my way over to what looks like flames dancing in the breeze coming through the window.

I walk up behind her, lifting her hair off her neck as she spins around to see who is touching her.

"Do you mind?" she asks, hand on her hip that is cocked out to the left. She is full of attitude, and I get the feelings she is going to be a wild ride in bed.

"I'm Mike."

"I don't give a fuck who you are," she snaps back. "Touch me again and you won't have a fucking hand."

"Mike... This is Butcher's girl."

"You're beautiful. Butcher is a lucky man. I didn't mean any disrespect."

Her pale, perfect skin turns rosy. "Thank you, no harm done." She turns to walk away.

"Are you insane? Butcher didn't get his name from being a nice guy."

"I know. Her red hair reminded me of someone I used to know." I need to get a grip. *Why is Rosie filling my mind?* Damn what I want to do to her sexy, foul mouth and the rest of her perfect little body. "Where's this job at? I need some funds." I get my head back into the job.

"I'm not so sure you're the right person for the job, Mikey."

"What the fuck do you mean? Don't be jerking me around, Duke."

"I'm trying to keep you from getting gutted. The job is snatching a few people and delivering them."

"Easy enough. What'd they do, fuck someone over?" I take a drink of the beer that was handed to me.

"Something like that." Duke's eyes grow wide as he looks behind me over my shoulder. "Be cool, Mikey."

I slowly turn to see what he's looking at. Headed in my direction is the beautiful redhead I had just pissed off; she hangs on the arm of the very large, FBI most-wanted, Butcher.

"Is this him?" Butcher asks his girlfriend. She doesn't say anything, just nods her head at him. "Did you tell my girl she was beautiful?"

"I actually said Butcher is a lucky man, the 'you are beautiful' came after." I wait for his giant fist to smash into my face.

"Do you usually go around complimenting women that belong to other men?"

"No, but I do believe if a woman is beautiful, it is disrespectful not to tell her so."

Butcher laughs this deep belly laugh. "Grab a beer and follow me." He walks away.

I follow him to a table at the back of the room. He motions for me to have a seat across from him. Instead, I take the one next to him, not wanting to have my back to a room filled with Disciples.

"That's not the chair I told you to take," Butcher tells me.

"You're right, it's not. I don't turn my back on anyone."

Butcher nods his head in agreement. "Duke says you're

looking for some work. I've done some checking on you. You have a good history at doing what's necessary, and then getting out of town for a while."

I don't say anything; I just let him talk.

"I need some people, quietly and quickly, brought to me. You will get ten thousand per person." He takes a drink of his beer, watching me for a response.

"Dead or alive?"

"Alive."

I whisper to him, "All at once or one at a time?"

"Has to be in a specific order. It's going to become more difficult with each one. The cops are going to become a big problem."

"Then we raise the price by five for each one or no deal. How many total?"

"Ten."

"Rival club?"

"Jury."

"Damn, that's one way to teach them." I hold my beer up to him. "You are a creative son of a bitch."

Butcher laughs and clinks his beer to mine. "Wait a minute, why only ten?" I cautiously ask.

"I've handled two on my own."

"So, you have jurors one and two?" I push him to answer.

"No." He doesn't admit to anything. "Here's your list and information on each. Duke is out from now on. He gets a grand for finding you and that's it. He isn't to know anything else." I reach out to take the envelope from him, he keeps a hold of it. "Fuck me over and they will never find all of you."

"Got it. I don't give a fuck what you're up to. I'm just

wanting some fast cash to get the fuck out of town." I look around the room. "You'll never lay eyes on me again."

He let's go of the envelope. I open it, taking a quick peek inside. "Thanks for the beers. I'll be in touch." I don't say anything to anyone else, I walk straight to the door to pick up my guns and knife, before exiting.

I would have loved to go straight to the station, but I know damn well I'm being tailed by more than a couple of the Disciples. So, I go to my apartment. I keep checking out the window to make sure no one is outside. I take out the phone from behind the headboard. I check in, letting the station know I have made contact with the target and photos will be coming. We need to come up with a game plan as to protecting the jurors and finding K.D.

An hour later, there's a knock on my door. "Come on, Mikey, open the door. I'm horny."

As soon as I hear the last words, I know it's Paula Barrott, an undercover unit in sex crimes. We have worked together several times and relieved each other's stress even more times.

I jerk the door open without a shirt on and the top button of my jeans undone. I pull her hard against me, kissing her as if I haven't seen her in forever. I'm not going to lie and say we haven't used each other to get by when we were undercover.

Working in these conditions gets lonely. She brings me information, and I do the same for her. We can get each other out of jams when needed, or when we have been away too long, the other is a warm body and a dose of reality to keep us from losing ourselves to this life. She's a reminder that I'm still a decent human.

Paula jumps into my arms, wrapping her legs around my

waist. I cup her ass as I kick the door closed behind us. I'm in no hurry to put her down after the run in with Butcher's girl today. My dick went hard as soon as I heard Paula's voice.

She is the first to break our kiss and loosens her legs from my waist, wiggling free until she stands in front of me. Instead of seeing long black hair, which she normally wears when she's undercover, she is wearing a long auburn-colored wig.

"What's with the hair color?" I ask her. Taking a step back, I fasten my jeans after adjusting my cock out of the way.

"I was watching the camera when you fucked up and touched the redhead. So, I thought I would play into it in case it came up again, and you needed a cover." She sits down on the couch, pulling papers out of her purse. "Want to talk about what that was about?"

I flop down on the couch, putting my feet up on the coffee table. "I don't know what the fuck happened. I saw the redhead and couldn't get Rosie out of my head."

"Rosie? Isn't she Macy's friend that runs the shop for her?" She turns on the couch, pulling her legs up under her to face me. "When did the two of you become an item?"

"We aren't. She ran into me at the NA meeting and is my sponsor."

"Mike, that's natural to get the hots for someone trying to help you. Besides, I've seen her. I'd fuck her." She reaches over and smacks me in the chest. "Do you think she would be up for a threesome?"

I can't help but laugh at the question. "I should know better than to discuss Rosie with your kinky ass." *Now I'm going to have some excellent ideas to beat off to tonight,* I think to myself.

Paula climbs across the couch and on to my lap, straddling

my hips. She wiggles back and forth. "Come on, Mike, you can't tell me you don't like the idea of watching me slowly undress Rosie while you sit there and watch."

She raises her shirt as she describes what she would do, "I lift her shirt, revealing her pale tattooed skin, then run my hands over the perfect canvas. Her head falls back as I tease and pull on her taut nipples. I wonder if they are pierced. Hmm… I hope they are." Paula is doing to herself everything she speaks about doing to Rosie.

My cock tries to break free of the confines of my jeans. I'm so hard it becomes painful to have Paula grind on me. My hands go to her ass, covered by a thin pair of cutoff jeans. She raises off of me, and I undo the front of the shorts. Sliding my hands under her tank top, I pull it over her head. I waste no time pulling the chain hanging from a barbell through each of her luscious nipples, which are standing at full attention. Cupping her ass, I stand to carry her into the bedroom.

"Wait, don't forget the play toys." She grabs her bag.

"I love it when you come prepared."

"Baby, I'm always prepared and ready. We both need to have some fun. So do your best." She clamps down on my nipple with her teeth, causing my dick to try to bust through the zipper of my jeans.

I moan loudly and toss her on the bed, face down. After jerking off her shorts, I'm very happy to see she is bare underneath. Without warning, I draw my hand back and quickly smack her ass—full force, five times— leaving my handprint fully defined on her plump cheek.

"Paula, what's your safe word?"

She doesn't answer. I undo my belt and rip it from my

jeans. "I'm going to ask you one last time. What are your safe words?"

"Fuck you," is the only thing I hear.

Whack! The sound of leather meeting her bare skin fills the air. Paula still doesn't say a word. She really wants to play tonight.

I walk to the other side of the bed to be closer to her head and lean down to whisper, "I'm going to stop playing and leave the room if you don't answer the question. Is that what you want?"

"Purple and yellow." Tears begin to fill her eyes. "Sir, please don't stop. I need this," she begs. "Please, Sir, punish me so I can please you."

I run my hand down her hair, then open her bag to get out items, putting each one on the dresser. I'm not saying a word to her as I do so. I'm very happy to see beads.

I pour some lube on them and walk back to the bed. I lift her ass in the air until she is on her knees. I start with the smallest bead on the end of the string and push them inside of her until the tenth and largest bead fills her vagina. The mixture of the lube and her own juices have her lips glistening with moisture.

"Hold still. I want you to count for me. Do you understand?"

"Yes, Sir."

"Do you know why you're being punished?"

"For turning Sir on to thoughts he shouldn't be thinking while he is working."

"That's right." I draw the belt back and bring it down on her perfect apple-shaped pale ass.

"One," she says, her legs quivering.

I do it again, lower so it will push the beads into her further as the leather meets her skin. "Oh yes, two." She moans.

I slip a finger between her folds and quickly pull the beads from her, causing her to come undone. I have removed my jeans, coating my cock in her juice, and line up with her anal opening.

Paula tenses.

"Breathe, I'm not going to hurt you."

I coat a finger, first pushing past her tightened cords. I slowly insert a second and begin to turn them back and forth as I move them in and out. Paula's muscles relax as she begins to push back against my hand, wanting me to go deeper. I remove my fingers and insert the head of my cock. I don't move to give her time to adjust.

"You're in control, Paula. You handle how deep you want me. How fast you want me." I reach under her and flick her taut clit, causing her to jump and push back against me. Taking me all into her. She is so tight, clamping down on me. I'm about to come undone.

"I have to move," she tells me.

She slides away from me then pushes back, burying me deep. The more she does that the more I play with her clit. Every time she buries herself, she clamps down, trying to milk my cock. She rolls her shoulders back and drops her head down. I'm coming. I take control, grabbing her hips and begin to pound in and out of her.

Paula's body shakes. She yells out, in almost a scream,

before collapsing on her stomach on the bed. I remove myself from her body.

"Are you okay, baby?" I ask her.

"Oh, my God. We have to do that again," she says with a chuckle.

"We will, but not right now. You lay there while I take care of you." I go get a warm cloth to wash her and take the after-care lotion from her bag and apply it to the red welts on her skin from the belt.

I bring her some juice to drink, giving her a few sips before climbing in bed with her. She curls up to my side where I wrap her in my arms.

She looks up at me with her big brown eyes. "You really have it bad for Rosie, don't you?"

"Why do you say that?" I try to avoid her eyes.

She winces as she raises up to climb onto my lap. The pain in her eyes makes me feel guilty. "Don't ruin what was almost perfect, Mike. The sting, causes a hum in my clit."

"What do you mean *almost* perfect?" I try to change the subject.

"We both know you were pretending you were fucking Rosie instead of me."

"I'm really a fucking prick, aren't I?"

"Well, in all fairness, I started it with the talk of the threesome." She begins to grind on my semi-hard cock.

"Paula, you need to rest for a little while." I grip her hips, trying to hold them in one place. I know damn well we aren't close to being over for the night.

"I want to explore this threesome some more." She smiles.

"Since when do you like to talk so much?" I ask, holding her hips against my hard cock.

"I'm trying new things this evening, and hopefully, trying a new redhead in the future with you. This position would be good. You, buried deep in me. Your mouth licking, tasting every inch of her, while I get to kiss her and explore that petite tight body with my hands and mouth."

Without giving her a warning, I lift her and set her down on the tip of my cock. Putting my hands on her shoulders, I push her down so she takes me in as far as she can.

Paula instantly begins to cum.

"Oh, you're not going to be finished that easy," I tell her. "You wanted to play this game so now we are going to play."

I lift her off my cock and bring her to my face. I begin to lap up all her juices. I touch her clit, and it's as if electrical volts shoot through her body. She's really turned on. I suck her clit in and scrape my teeth along it.

Paula's body shivers as I do that. I continue to suck and flick it gently with my tongue; it grows to a hard nub in my mouth as I bite my teeth across her clit again. The juices flow from her. Her knees quiver as I hold her body up. I keep lapping at her as she tries to escape my assault.

I won't give up until I can coax another orgasm from her. When it hits, she falls back on the bed. I have to change my position on her. I grab the remote-control dildo from the dresser and slide it in and out of her to fully coat it. I ease the mechanism into her tender anus. Putting Paula's ankle's up on my shoulders, as I'm on my knees between her legs, I fill her core and turn on the dildo.

"Oh, my gawd! Please don't stop!" Paula grabs onto my arms and pulls me to her with more force.

I'm thrusting as hard as I can. I explode my wad inside her and collapse beside her. She still quivers. "Shut it off!" she screams.

"Fuck, I'm sorry." I grab the remote I dropped, shut the dildo off, and gently remove it from inside her.

"No talking, sleep." I don't say a thing just pull the covers up over the two of us and hold her in my arms.

* * *

I WAKE AND THE ROOM IS COMPLETELY DARK. I COVER PAULA as I slide out of bed. I pick up all evidence of the event that happened earlier and take the items to the bathroom to clean them. When I'm done, I jump in the shower.

I pull on some jeans without fastening the top. I put the toys back into her bag before walking to the kitchen. I put on some coffee. I pull out my personal phone from where I have it hidden and send a quick text to Macy.

"I'm doing good. Don't worry. Be in touch when I can. Love you."

I debate about sending one to Rosie, then I think why not? She's my sponsor and worried about me. My dick twitches at the thought of everything Paula and I discussed.

"Rosie, I'm good, not using. I do have one problem... I can't quit thinking about a certain redhead covered in tattoos. They aren't pure thoughts."

I hit send.

I put the phone back into its hiding spot. I'm pouring myself coffee, as a pair of arms wrap around my waist. I reach up and grab another cup, filling it full of black coffee. I turn around and Paula snuggles into my chest.

"I expected you to sleep a couple more hours." I brush the hair out of her face.

"Nah, I'm good. Nice and tender in all the right spots and some new ones too." She raises up on her tiptoes and gently kisses my lips. "I have to go under tonight. A new guy downtown is cutting up girls. I'm going to see if I can give them a hand in drawing him out. Seems like you're not the only one that has a thing for petite redheads."

"Wait, what do you mean he has a thing for redheads? Where is he hunting?"

"He's downtown, around the soup kitchen. Don't worry he's about six blocks east of the tattoo shop. If something changes, I'll let you know." She tries to pull her hand out of mine.

"Watch yourself. Stay in touch with me." I pull her back against me. "I'm serious."

"I will, Mike." She squeezes my hand. "We have a tattoo artist to win over." Paula winks before walking out the door, closing it behind her.

I pull the hidden phone out again, quickly type another text.

"I just got word it's not safe around the soup kitchen. Please stay out of the area. Explain later."

CHAPTER SEVEN

ROSIE

As I sit on the couch in Macy's office and flip through an old photo album filled with photos of us, I'm consumed by anxiety and I'm not sure why. Oh, hell... Who am I kidding? I know why. I can't quit thinking about Mike. I haven't been this anxious since I quit meth over four years ago.

I know it's not a good comparison, but we had a good time together that night, a year ago. I could easily fall for a guy like Mike. My past history with men has never been good. I have the battle scars to prove some of my bad decisions.

It started when I had just turned eighteen and out on my own; my mom threw me out of the house because I told her I didn't like her newest boyfriend living with us.

I met Steven, he had a car, was twenty-seven, gorgeous, and always had a wad of cash in his pocket. He was a small-time dealer that liked to fuck and party.

Then one night, he decided I should fuck him and a few of his friends. When I refused, he beat me and left me for dead. This landed me in the hospital.

I met Macy that night. She had been there visiting a friend when she saw me. She came into my room and started talking to me. She told me if I needed a job to come by the tattoo shop and I could clean up. Macy became a big sister to me. I met a few more losers over the year until I realized it was time to take a break from the dating scene.

I had began learning how to tattoo by watching Macy and some of the others that would stop in to meet with a client as they passed through the city.

I kept practicing my artwork, even taking a few classes during the day at the local community college. Then Macy made me an apprentice and the manager of the shop.

I eventually grew my own client base, and here I am today, not exhausted after finishing the full back piece today. I love what I do, and Macy and I have been slammed lately. We are actually looking for a fifth artist for the shop.

We've interviewed four people this week; we have one more that is coming in tomorrow.

I reached out to Don, K.D.'s husband, and asked if there was anything I could do to help out. He asked me if I would draw up a few fliers for him to print and share around town.

Macy and I drew them, printed two hundred fifty each and Don picked them up just before closing.

I can't imagine going through what he is. I remember watching David when his brother kidnapped Macy. Our world had come to a stop as we didn't know what hell he was putting her through.

Macy tried to get me to come home with her and have dinner with her and David. I wasn't up to it. I need to get home to the quiet, where I can relax and think.

I need to try to figure out why I've been thinking of Mike nonstop since he left. I know I'm worried about his safety, but he's a good cop. There's something more, and I'm not sure what it is.

I take a shower and climb into bed, without bothering to put anything on. A few minutes later I'm a sleep.

* * *

I'VE BEEN TOSSING AND TURNING ALL NIGHT; FOR SOME REASON, I just can't stay asleep. My mind is filled with thoughts of Mike. I look at the time when my phone dings. I have a text from Mike.

They aren't pure thoughts. What does that mean?

I run my hands down my body and think of Mike's hands roaming over me. My nipples grow rigid. I hook my fingernail in the hoop piercing, a gentle pull causes a unique pressure to build, not only in my nipples but also between my legs.

I get out of bed and go to the corner of my room to get the new accessory I've only used once. Tonight, seems like the perfect night to try it again. I call it my rocking horse, a black mechanical horse with a horn and a dildo. Motioning back and forth causes the dildo to thrust in and out.

I climb on and slowly lower down on to the dildo, then slowly begin rocking back and forth. Using my right hand, I rub my clit at the same time, imagining Mike's hands on my body and his mouth on my clit. The faster I rock, the harder I get fucked. In no time, I cum, my juices coating everything.

As I climb off the horse, I say aloud, "Best six hundred dollars I have ever spent." I get some Clorox wipes and clean up the toy, then go to the bathroom and clean myself up.

After, I put on some clothes and drink some coffee. Maybe I can get some sketches in before meeting Macy at the gym. I always have a renewed energy after a good orgasm. That is the reason I spent the money on the horse. A friend of mine had one and she let me try it out. I was sold after the first time.

We plan on having a horse race party with a bunch of our girlfriends one night. I'm looking forward to it. I wonder what Mike would think if he knew I was bisexual. Would he still be interested?

My phone dings again. *"Area around soup kitchen isn't safe. Stay away. Will explain later."* That's an ominous message.

Mike would never put me in danger. So, I decide to follow what the message says until I get a chance to talk to Mike.

* * *

I'M SO ENGROSSED IN SKETCHING; I DON'T REALIZE IT'S TIME to meet Macy at the gym. My phone rings. "Where are you?" she asks.

"I'm sorry, I didn't sleep well, so I have been drawing and lost track of time. I'll meet you at the shop."

"Are you sure?" Macy asks, concerned.

"Totally sure. You go, I'll see you after." I put away my art supplies and go to the bedroom to get ready for work. I can't help seeing the horse in the corner and wanting to go for another ride.

I decide to strap on my wearable vibrator shaped like a butterfly against my clit as I lube the dildo. I climb on and ease myself down. I turn on the butterfly and the hum begins to gently vibrate as I slowly begin to rock back and forth. The excitement builds with each thrust as I jerk the handle harder and harder each time. I am going as fast as I can when the orgasm hits. My legs to kick out straight, pushing the dildo up as far up in me as it will go.

"Holy fuck." I climb off the toy. This can become a very fun way to spend time at home. I jump in the shower after cleaning up.

When I pull up to the shop, I do what I need to do to get ready to open, then walk up to the front to open the blinds and flip the sign. As soon as I open the blinds, there is a petite woman with blue eyes, long dark hair in a braid. She has a beautiful smile and a body that aches to be touched. She wears a wife beater T-shirt that has been cut to make it even lower, hip hugging cutoffs that show the bottom of her ass cheeks.

"Welcome to the shop. How can I help you?" I ask, holding the door open for her, then follow her back to the counter, enjoying the view as we go.

"Hi, wow! What a great shop. Mike told me about it, but he didn't really do it justice. You're Rosie, he described you perfectly. I thought he had to be lying about how gorgeous you are." She looks my body up and down without being uncomfortable with what she is doing. "I'm Paula." She holds her hand out to me.

"Mike... Mike who?"

"Oh, I'm sorry." She pulls out her badge and shows me. "Mike Anderson. We work together."

"So, you're a cop like Mike. That's cool. What division do you work in?" I ask, hoping to learn how Mike is doing.

"I'm in sex crimes. I've worked with Mike a few times. As a matter of fact, I saw him last night," she says with a smile on her face.

I would love to question her more about seeing Mike, but I have work to do. "Paula, were you wanting to set an appointment today?"

"I am. I want a full sleeve."

"When are you wanting to get started? I would prefer to get as much of the outline done in one sitting that you can handle. That way everything stays symmetrical."

"Do you have any time available, say Saturday?" She leans against the counter, pushing her breasts up.

I flip through my appointment book. "I'm clear after ten a.m., if that will work?"

"That's perfect. Macy wouldn't happen to be in, would she?" Paula asks, looking around the shop.

"Not yet, do you know Macy?"

She turns back to face me. "No, I haven't had the pleasure. Mike just wanted me to make sure the two of you knew he was doing fine. I promised him I would make sure."

"Macy will appreciate hearing it, as I do. What designs are you wanting on your sleeve?"

"I want it to be about the beauty of women. I appreciate the beauty of the human form. I'm bisexual. I have several pictures I can send you and you can draw something up. We can meet up to go over it if you like, maybe get dinner or a drink?"

"Dinner sounds good. What if I cook?" Reaching up, I push loose hairs behind her ear.

A smile breaks out on her face. "This week needs to hurry and fly by. Can I have your number to send you the photos?"

"Hopefully, that's not the only reason you want my number. I'm looking forward to hearing from you." I come around to the front of the counter. "I'll walk you out."

When we get to the door, I open it for her. "It's been nice to meet you, Paula. I can't wait to see you on Friday."

"Bye, Rosie." She leans over and gently kisses me on the lips. "Till Friday."

"So now I know why you didn't meet me at the gym. Whose she?" Macy stands behind me, grinning.

"That is Paula. We are going out Friday, and I'm doing a sleeve on her Saturday."

"Wait, what?"

"What's wrong with that?"

"It's been a long time since you have moved this quickly, Rosie."

"Did you see her? She is fucking hot. Why do I always need to take it slow and be the one that does everything the right way. Maybe, just maybe, I want to have some fun. If it doesn't work out, so be it." I start setting up everyone's workstations. "I didn't realize I had to have your opinion to live my life, Macy."

"Hey... What the hell, Rosie? Where is all this coming from?"

"Fuck, I don't know. Your brother has my thoughts all

fucked up. He's never showed any interest until the other night."

"If you're interested in Mike, then what's up with this with Paula? I love you like a sister, Rosie, you know this, but Mike is still my brother."

"I get it. I really do. Did you ever tell Mike I'm bisexual?"

"Not that I know of. Why does it matter?"

"It doesn't. I'm not sure why I asked. Let's get to work. I'm done discussing my nonexistent sex life." I wipe down the chairs.

Macy walks up behind me and gives me a hug. "I thought you bought the rocking horse to help with that problem." She grins at me. "Doesn't it work?"

"It worked great this morning." I can't help laughing as I hold up two fingers to her.

Macy laughs. "Is horse riding becoming a new habit?"

"Yes, and I might need to run home for lunch as well." We're both laughing as the other two tattoo artists come in, followed by the start of the morning's clients.

The rest of the day is packed with nonstop clients and people coming in to book appointments in the near future. I have an hour break between clients, so I check my phone and there are several texts from Paula. She wants a sunrise over the beach. Women in different forms of dress from bikinis to formals, ending with a sun set at the wrist.

Grabbing a bottle of water out of the fridge, I go into Macy's office with my sketch pad and set out drawing an idea for Paula's sleeve. The women are walking down a sidewalk as their age and clothing changes to represent different stages of life.

Macy comes in to let me know another client is here to see me. "Can I see what you've been working on?" she asks.

"It's only the outline, but what do you think?" I show it to her.

"Rosie, this is one of the best drawings I've seen you do. I can't wait to see it done."

Praise like that, coming from Macy, means the world to me. She is one of the best artists I've ever seen. People come from all over the world to have her work on them; that's why she has a six-month waiting period to get an appointment with her. "Thanks, Macy. I'll be right there." I start to clean up my pencils and sketch pad, then walk out into the shop.

It's buzzing with creative energy. All the chairs have clients in them, and the counter has a line of people waiting to be tended to. My client is here to add color to the outline we finished yesterday.

The day flies by. Every minute filled with something new. This is why I love being a tattoo artist. There is never a never a dull moment.

CHAPTER EIGHT

MIKE

I'm asked to come into the station, so we can devise a plan to capture Butcher and find the missing victim. We are looking through the photos when we realize the next juror is a kindergarten teacher, petite build, shoulder-length dark hair and fit.

"Fuck, I'm supposed to deliver a female to this mad man? What if we put her in protective custody and announce she has been killed in an accident?" I'm pacing the room as the door opens and the Federal Bureau of Investigation (FBI), and the Oklahoma State Bureau of Investigation (OSBI) enter the room to join in the meeting that is about to take place.

"We can send an undercover officer to replace her. That way we can track them back to where the Butcher is taking them," someone in the back of the room suggested.

"Butcher is not a dumb man. He will know right away if

that isn't the juror. He has done his homework on them. Our only chance to find K.D. Baker is to follow Butcher and pray he has kept him alive."

"Why do you think he's still alive?" I'm asks.

"Butcher is very adamant that they be brought to him in a specific order. He said if they had to be brought out of order, they would keep until their turn."

"I think we should see how he reacts to the news that juror number two is dead from a car wreck. See if this causes him to lead us to K.D. If anything, we have bought a day or two of time."

Chief agrees and sends undercover agent to pick up the juror and her family members. They will be taken directly out of town to some place safe for them all.

Within an hour, the juror and her family are safely tucked away at the expense of the Oklahoma judicial system. I can breathe for the moment, but I still can't shake the feeling something is going to go wrong with their choice.

I have on my tracker and my mic as I dial Butcher to let him know about the accident. It has taken us seven hours to put together a fake accident scene and newsreel to be shared on all stations. I'm at the scene in case he decides to make an appearance.

"Yeah?" he answers the phone

"Turn on the news. We have a problem."

"I don't like problems."

"I fucking don't either. This is a big one."

"What am I looking at?"

I answer, "Number two is in the car that is on its roof."

"Is she dead?"

"I'm going to try to get closer. Hold on." I walk through the crowd as they pull the juror through the window and cover her entire body with a white cloth before loading her in an ambulance that leaves without any sirens or lights. I walk away from the crowd and report into the phone what I just witnessed.

"FUCK!" The phone goes dead.

I jump on my bike and check my tracker for his location. I'm only five blocks from where he is. As I arrive, I see him jump into the black Dodge dually pickup he has been driving. I fall back to where I can follow him without him seeing me. The tracker I placed on his truck the other night seems to be working great.

We are headed east on Meridian. Butcher weaves in and out of traffic. With as many agencies we have watching him, we can all take turns keeping an eye on him. Some will jump off the road while another group jumps back on. This keeps Butcher from being able to identify anyone.

After fifteen minutes, he takes an exit toward Oak Street and continues south. The houses thin out as we approach the old racetrack that has been closed down for years. The only thing still standing is the building where the head mechanic worked. There are a few other empty buildings around there, but not many are still standing.

I park along the outside fence and watch as Butch walks into the mechanic's building. I call in my location, and I'm told to wait for backup that's not too far out, but I can't do that.

I still haven't figured out why he wants them brought to him in the order of their juror numbers. Maybe it's as simple as one, two, three. Keeping track of them is much easier if they're sequential. He's deadly, not exactly a criminal mastermind like Jack.

I creep up along the outside of the building. Butcher yells at someone inside. The second person has only muffled sounds. They aren't able to respond to what he is saying to them. I look inside a dirt-crusted window, but I'm unable to see anything other than a figure standing and one lying down.

This must be K.D.

Butcher is going to kill K.D. if I don't get in there to save him. I see a side door that isn't closed all the way and make my way into the dark building. I have to take a second to give my eyes a moment to adjust to the darkness.

Using a small flashlight I had in my pocket, I make my way to the right, careful not to trip and make noise. I'm outside a closed door when I hear Butcher:

"Stupid bitch had to ruin my plans. Now you are going to suffer for her as well." I hear a muffled scream as I send a text to tell my chief where I am in the building. I'm entering the room now.

K.D. Baker is strapped to the table in nothing but his boxers.

"POLICE, FREEZE! Drop it, Butcher. Put your hands up!" I yell as I kick through the door.

Butcher spins around, holding a knife in his hand. "You're a fucking cop."

"That's right. Take a step, and you'll die." I aim for his massive chest. There are only ten feet separating me and him. Butcher steps to me with the knife in his right hand as runs toward me.

I raise my gun a few inches and pull the trigger.

Butcher drops where he stands, blood spreading between his eyes and running onto the floor. I check for a pulse and kick the knife out of his hand.

I get on the phone to call for an ambulance for K.D. He has several slices over his body, each different in depth. Looking at the medical and mechanical tools that were on the counters surrounding the table that K.D. laid on was sickening. Different sizes of sharpened objects, from a surgeon's scalpel to a hatchet, are laid out for Butcher to use. The medics told me none of K.D.'s injuries were life-threatening.

The F.B.I. and O.S.B.I. all converge at the crime scene. The warehouse where Duke had taken me to meet Butcher has been raided and the remaining Disciples are in jail, including Duke for harboring a fugitive. When searching further into where K.D. was held, the head of the first missing juror had been discovered in a freezer in a garage.

* * *

IT'S MIDNIGHT WHEN I GO TO THE APARTMENT AND PICK UP ALL my stuff. I'm not spending another night here. I know what I want and who I want, so it's time I start going after it.

I pull up to the house when the garage door opens, and the garage light comes on. David stands there with Macy at his side in one of his oversized shirts.

"I'm home, if you'll still have me." I climb off the bike.

Macy runs to me. "Welcome home. Are you here to stay? Did you get him?"

"I got him," I answer, hugging her.

Macy steps back, and David pulls me into a brotherly hug. "It's good to have you home."

"What about K.D.? We've made fliers for Don to hang up. Rosie has been staying in touch with him."

"How do you know Don and K.D.?" I'm confused as to the relationship with Rosie, Macy, and the Bakers.

"K.D. is a client and friend of Rosie's. She has done his tats and even went to the club and watched his show before. They became friends."

"Come around more often, and you will know more." David punches me in the arm. "I've even been with the girls to the club."

"I plan on being around a lot from now on." I punch him back. "Damn, I act like I hurt my hand hitting him." I wonder if it's too late to send a text to Rosie. I pull my phone out and then put it back in my pocket.

"I bet she's still up sketching," Macy tells him. "She's starting a sleeve on a new client tomorrow."

"I'll catch her in the morning in case she's in bed. She's going to have a long day."

"Suit yourself. I'm glad your home Mike." She takes David's hand and begins to walk down the hall. "Night, little brother."

"Night." Fuck it. I send a quick text to Rosie.

"I'm home. I didn't want to call in case you were sleeping. Want to meet at the diner in the morning for breakfast?"

I start to hit send, then go back and edit my text to add:

"I've missed you."

CHAPTER NINE

ROSIE

I've been home long enough to make myself a glass of iced tea when my phone dings. *"What are you doing?"* It's Paula.

"I just got home. I was going to draw for a while. I'm not really tired."

"Would you be interested in some company? I don't mean to be pushy... I haven't quit thinking of you since I laid eyes on you."

"I agree. There was something between the two of us. Why don't you come over? We can talk about it."

We are only going to talk, I tell myself. Knowing damn well that's not at all what I had in mind. I send her my address.

Fifteen minutes later, there's a knock on my door. I look through the peephole to see Paula, dark hair loose around her shoulders, a spaghetti strap purple T-shirt on with nothing underneath. Leggings hug every curve of her perfectly shaped ass.

I step aside to let her in. "Welcome. Damn, you are gorgeous," I say as she walks through the door.

She looks over her shoulder at me with a sexy grin on her face. "Where do you want me?" she asks seductively.

"Right there works," I respond as she stops in front of the sofa and lifts her shirt over her head, revealing a pair of breasts that are muscular with their constricted nipples pointing at the sky. "Show me more," I command her.

Paula turns her back to me and slowly begins to draw down the leggings by hooking her fingers in the waistband. She watches me over her shoulder as she ever so slowly draws the material down. She steps her left leg out, then her right. She tosses her pants into the chair where she had tossed her top.

I move to her, wrapping her long dark hand around my hand. I pull her head to the side as I run my tongue up her neck and down the other side. I grip her ass cheek with my hand and squeeze.

Without thinking, I pull my hand back and smack it, causing a loud whack to echo throughout the room.

"Do you like that?" I ask as I draw back to do it again.

Paula spins around and knocks me to the floor. "No one said you get to be in charge, little one. You didn't ask me before you struck me. You just thought you had the right to do so." She wipes a tear from the side of my face. "I was all eager to play with you until you thought you were in charge. I thought you were going to be different, Rosie. I had plans for you and me. Maybe I'll still tell you." She brushes the hair out of my face.

"Too bad Mike won't be able to join us. He was so turned

on at the idea of the three of us together." She handcuffs me and begins to dress. "We are going to go somewhere much more private. This way, when we are playing, if you want to scream, you can and not disturb the neighbors." She pulls me to my feet and whispers in my ear, "I hope you scream. It's such a turn-on when they do." She jerks my chin until I'm facing her. "We are going to go outside and get in my car. If you make a noise and anyone comes out, they will die. Do you understand?"

I nod, not saying a word.

She grabs her bag, and we head out the door. She has put a jacket over my hands to cover the handcuffs in case someone looks out their door.

The door three houses down from me opens, and my neighbor steps out. "Rosie, girl, where are you off to this late?"

"You know me, I'm always up to something. Have a nice night. Don't wait up." I laugh, so does my neighbor.

"Not bad," Paula says as we exit the apartment building. She opens the front passenger door of her car. "He's still watching, so you better make it look good." She leans in and kisses me. I put on a show for his safety.

As I sit down in the seat, I see he has closed the blinds and his apartment is now dark. I hope he mentions this to Macy when she comes looking for me in the morning.

We drive for over an hour. We are outside of the city and close to a lake. I can smell the water and hear the waves lapping against the shore. "Where are we?" I ask, hoping she will answer my questions.

"We're at my parents' cabin. This way we can have some

fun without anyone disturbing us. There are no neighbors for ten miles away."

"You know, if you wanted to be in charge, all you had to do is say so. I'm a switch. I have no problem letting you take control. I'm up to having some fun with you. We didn't have to come this far out."

"Rosie, you aren't ready for the type of fun we are going to have."

We pull into a driveway with trees along both sides "Paula, do you always play so seriously? What about your tattoo?" I look out the window at the cabin she is pulling up to. "This is a beautiful home. I bet it was nice growing up here?"

"Shut the fuck up. You ask too many damn questions." She slams the car into park.

I remain quiet as she gets out and walks around to my door. Paula opens the door, pulling me up from the seat. I step out of the way of the door, and she closes it, shoving me back against the car. Her lips are on mine, grinding against my mouth. I try to slow her down as she reaches up and grabs a handful of my hair. "I'm in control."

"I'm not trying to fight you. Let's go inside where we can get more comfortable. Maybe you can make it to where I can use at least one of my hands?" I lean into her neck, running my tongue up to her ear.

Paula doesn't argue with me as she leads me toward the back door. We enter; to say the cabin is gorgeous is an understatement. Twelve-foot ceilings, a rock fireplace at one end of the room. There's a full moon allowing me to see the lake through the wall of windows at the front of the house.

"Paula, this is amazing. Thank you for bringing me here. I

can't think of a more romantic place to explore each other's body." I turn, walking up to her. I decide to submit to her since she wants to be in charge. Hopefully, I will get a chance to escape when her guard is down. I drop to my knees and put my hands on my lap, keeping my eyes down.

"That's what I want to see." She puts her hand on my head, running her hand down my hair. She raises my chin to look at her. "I can promise you the next few days are some that you aren't going to forget anytime soon."

A shiver of fear runs down my spine. "My, my, aren't you full of excitement."

"Stand up," she tells me. I stand still, looking at the floor. She uncuffs me, pulling me against her.

"I want to taste you. Get on the bar." Paula pats the breakfast bar.

I get on the barstool and climb over to the bar.

"Raise your ass and take off your jeans." I do as I'm told. It's hard for me to admit, but I'm turned on by the direction things are going. Paula hasn't done anything to hurt me. Maybe this is some sort of scene, her version of foreplay. I have done scenes with other Doms far more dangerous than this.

Paula stands on the rails of the barstool and tells me to raise my hands over my head. I do so, and she cuffs my wrists to a hook above my head.

My knees are spread, and zip ties are put around each of my ankles and through eye hooks in the bar. She pulls out her phone and starts taking pictures of me like this. "Look at me," Paula demands.

I do as I'm told.

Paula scoots my hips close to her face and buries her face in my core, lapping at my center and causing my clit to throb.

I begin to squirm, trying to rub myself against her face.

She bites the inside of my thigh, causing me to cry out. "Don't move."

Paula licks and nips at my clit until I cry out as I cum. My head falls back as my legs shake, trying to make her stop. Her assault continues until a second wave of orgasm. She gets up and walks behind me into the kitchen, acting as if nothing just happened.

My shirt is pulled back away from my skin as she takes a knife and cuts the back of it open. Paula walks back to the front of me and does the same. I hold my breath as she cuts through the neckline and nicks my jaw with the blade. Blood slowly drips and runs down my chest.

"My gawd, you are something. I can see why he wants you. By the time I'm done with you, he won't even be able to look at you."

I'm not sure who Paula is referring to, but I'm starting to worry she has me confused with someone else. I have to find a way out of here. I look around the room, trying to see if there is anything obvious I can use as a weapon.

"I really wish things could have been different, Rosie. You and I could have had loads of fun together, but he wants you more than he does me. He used me while he pretended I was you."

"Now I'm going to use you and make him watch, until he realizes I'm the one he wants."

"Who are you talking about?" I ask her. "I don't know who you are talking about. I thought you and I were going to have a good time together." I try to get free. "Paula, I'm only interested in you."

Paula has walked out of the room.

"Paula, where are you?"

Footsteps coming down the hall, and a phone rings behind me.

"You should have chosen me. Now she's mine. Enjoy the show, Mike."

"Mike? What does Mike have to do with this?" I ask Paula. "What show are you talking about? Talk to me, Paula. Tell me what's going on."

I hear the leather swish through the air before I feel the bite of it across my back. "Agh," I scream out in pain. Again, the leather bites my skin over and over.

* * *

I must have passed out. I wake the room is dark, Paula is nowhere to be found. "Paula, Paula… where are you?" There is no answer, and no sound that she is still in the house.

Fear begins to rise. This isn't some sex scene. I'm never going to get out of here. I try to pull my arms free; they are heavy, and all the blood has drained from them from being held over my head for so long. The metal of the cuffs has rubbed my skin raw at my wrists. When pulling on my ankles trying to free them, the zip tie slices through my skin.

CHAPTER TEN

MIKE

It feels good to be back home again. *I can't wait to surprise Rosie in the morning,* I think as I lie in bed. Just as I'm dozing off to sleep, my phone vibrates with a message. I must still have it on silence from earlier.

I see I have a missed call from Paula. I pick up the phone and hit play. "You should have chosen me. Now she's mine. Enjoy the show, Mike." I hear Paula say as I see pictures of Rosie… naked and tied up on some kind of bar. The sound of leather biting skin tears through the quiet as Paula swings the strip of leather against Rosie's pale skin.

I study the background, and I don't know the place where Paula has her. I jump out of bed and put on my jeans, pulling a shirt over my head as I bang on Macy and David's bedroom door.

"Cover up. I'm coming in." I barge inside and aim straight

for my sister. "Macy, do you know if Rosie has a cabin somewhere?"

"Mike, what the hell?" She pulls the sheet up to her chest. "What the fuck are you doing?"

"Answer me: does Rosie have a log cabin?"

"No, why? It's three in the morning. What is going on? Is Rosie in some kind of trouble? You need to tell me now!" Macy yells at me.

I look helplessly around the room, trying to find something that will give me a clue where she is being held. Macy grabs David's shirt, pulling it on. "Mike, what the hell is going on?"

"I received a video of Rosie being tied up."

Macy grabs her phone and dials Rosie. "No answer." She walks up to me. "Rosie met a woman the other day. They hit it off, and Rosie was interested in her; she has been working on a sleeve design for her. She was very specific in what she wanted on the sleeve. She even emailed Rosie photos to incorporate."

"Did you see the woman or meet her?"

"I got a glimpse of her as she was leaving the shop that day. She wasn't the normal type Rosie usually goes for. On the petite side, long dark hair in a braid down her back. Even though she was small, she walked like she could hold her own if she needed to."

"Why do you think that?" Mike questions me.

"Let's go to the kitchen and put some coffee on," Macy tells me.

We walk out of the bedroom into the kitchen, and David is standing there, pouring three mugs of coffee. "I knew you would want coffee, and we're going to need it to find Rosie."

"Thank you," I tell David as he hands me coffee. "I think I

know who has her. Macy, if I show you a photo, do you think you could recognize her if you see a photo of her?"

"I can try?"

I open my phone and go to photos. I have several pictures of Paula and I over the years. Opening the newest one, that's only a few months old, I show it to Macy.

"Who is this, Mike?" she asks me.

"Just look at the photo, Macy." I flip to the next picture of Paula. She stands between me and another detective, her hand on her holster.

"She's a cop?"

"Macy, look at the fucking picture, please!" I slam my cup down, and coffee goes everywhere. David jumps up and gets between Macy and me.

I push David out of the way, pulling Macy into a hug. "I'm sorry, Macy. I'm going nuts thinking this is my fault. I have to know if that's Paula that you saw before I go to the station and blow up her career."

"Let me see the pictures again." She flips through several pictures of me and Paula. She stops on one of Paula alone. "Mike, she had this shirt on when she was at the shop and her hair was just like this. It's her." I take a step back from Macy. "Mike, what has she done to her?"

"I'll be in touch. I have to get to the station and see if I can find them. I promise to call as soon as I know where she is." I give Macy a quick hug before running back to my room, pulling on my boots, and running out the door.

I call the Chief and ask him to meet me at the station, telling him we have a problem with one of the officers. I give him a rundown of what has happened since Paula came to see me at the safe house. I didn't leave anything out. I told him if I had to face disciplinary actions, then so be it. Getting Rosie back is all that matters.

I play the video for him. He calls in Paula's sergeant and has her phone records pulled. He also ordered any property records in Paula's name to be pulled or any other family members.

As we are going through all the documentation, my phone dings with another text message. I open it, seeing it's from Paula. It's another video. The techs connect my phone, so it plays on the big screen in the room.

There's Rosie's, hands still cuffed above her head. Her face is tear streaked and there are red marks all over her body. I tell them to zoom in on her chest. I cringe when I realize the red marks are slices in Rosie's skin. "Fuck! We have got to find where she has her, fucking now! Doesn't anyone have anything?"

I calm down and take my phone from the tech to dial Paula even though I don't expect her to answer. I'm amazed when she does. "Paula?"

"Mike, I was wondering when I was going to hear from you." She combs her hair down with her hand.

"Why are you doing this, Paula? Rosie didn't do anything to you. You could have taken me instead of her anytime." I'm trying to keep her on the line so we can get a location. "Paula, you know I care about you; why would you do this? I thought we had something good. Are you really going to let my sober coach come between what we had together?"

"You want her instead of me. I watched you almost blow your case because you saw red hair."

I'm watching Rosie as Paula stands in front of her talking to me and holding the camera. Rosie mouths something in the background. I hand a note to the tech to zoom in on Rosie.

"Can anyone read lips? Get me someone that can read lips!" I'm whispering at no one in particular, so Paula doesn't hear.

Another officer comes running in. "I can," she says with confidence and watches the screen. "It looks like Eufaula Lake Cabins," the officer announces in a low voice.

"Paula, I was thinking of you with the red hair. Remember when we went to the picnic with the rest of the crew, and you wore the red wig? You were gorgeous. We had so much fun that day and even more that night. You have to remember that night, don't you?"

I get in my car and head to Eufaula. My phone is still patched through to the station so they can keep an eye on the situation I'm walking into.

"I know you're on your way, Mike. The question is... will you be here in time?"

"In time for what, Paula?" I smash the gas pedal to the floor, afraid of what Paula will do to Rosie. I have my sirens going on the patrol car I took from an unsuspecting officer.

"Let's see who you really care for?" Paula carries the phone over to Rosie. "Do you want to say something to Mike before you die?" She grabs her hair, jerking Rosie's head back, raising her face up to the camera.

Paula kisses Rosie roughly. "Rosie, did you know Mike fucked me while fantasizing about you. I was talking about the three of us having a threesome while he was buried deep inside of me."

Tears run down Rosie's cheeks as she tries to pull her head out of Paula's grasp.

"Awe, Mike, I don't think she's happy with you anymore. Look at the tears. I'm done talking for a while, Mike. I'll see you soon. Rosie and I are going to have some more fun. Before I hang up, Mike, I thought you might want to know: her pussy is just as sweet as we thought it would be."

"FUCK!" I scream at the top of my lungs. My phone rings and I answer it right away.

"Anderson." The tech on the other end of the line was able to trace Paula's phone and get me an address. It's a cabin owned by Paula's parents. They were killed several years ago in an accident. Local authorities have been notified and are on their way to the property.

They have been informed not to make a move until I get there. I'm within fifteen minutes of arriving at the address when my phone begins to ring. "I don't know if you're going to make it in time, Mike. Rosie isn't looking good."

I see something out the corner of my eye: an orange glow fills the sky and grows. My heart beats erratically as I realize it's a fire. The police radio goes off calling for fire and paramedics due to a house fire. The address of the report is the cabin where Rosie is being held captive.

I fly around the corner to see the back of the cabin on fire. My car comes sliding to a stop as I jump out and run to the front door, pulling my gun. Other officers follow my lead and cover the other areas around the house.

"Paula, I'm coming in." I reach up and check the doorknob. To my surprise, it's open. Two officers follow me through the door. "Paula, let's get you and Rosie outside, where it's safe, so we can talk," I try to coax her out. I walk further into the house, finally seeing her and Rosie in the hallway, the flames only about five feet behind them.

"Paula, can we go outside away from the fire? Let me help you get outside with Rosie."

"You only want her because she isn't broken. You used to want me that way."

"Paula, you're not broken. What are you talking about? I don't understand." I take a step closer to them. Rosie is barely standing on her own, fear filling her eyes. There is a lot of blood running down the side of her head.

Paula looks behind her and sees the flames getting closer. "I couldn't be without you. I had to do it so that you would come back to me, Mike. It was the only way I knew for you to come back."

"Paula, come on let's get out of here. I don't want to see you or Rosie get hurt. We can go outside where no one will bother us, and we can be alone and talk about everything." I'm slowly stepping closer to them.

Rosie can feel the heat of the fire and struggles to get free in Paula's arms. I can see the knife in her hand cutting Rosie's skin along her breast with each struggle. Panic has taken over, and Rosie doesn't feel the pain of the cuts any longer.

I know SWAT has joined us in the house. If I can get close enough to pull Rosie free of Paula's arms, I can get her safely out of the house and the other officers can take down Paula.

Taking another step closer, I have one shot at getting Rosie's attention. "Rosie, stop! Look at me!" I yell at her.

At that moment, both women stop moving and have their eyes on me. Paula's grip loosens on Rosie as I rush forward and jerk her out of Paula's arms. One shot is all it takes to put an end to Paula's terror.

I scoop Rosie up in my arms and carry her out to the waiting ambulance. She doesn't want to let go of my neck as I try to lay her on the gurney for the paramedics to begin working on her. "Rosie, I'm right here. Please let them help you. I'm going to call Macy and let her know you're safe; she and David can meet us at the hospital."

I hear the whirl of a helicopter as it lands on the road. We push the gurney to meet the medical team running toward us. As they start to strap Rosie down, she fights them.

"Honey, it's all right. Hold my hand, I'm going with you. I'll be with you the entire ride." She looks at me, really looks at me, and the dam of emotion breaks. They give her some medication to help calm her down and ease the pain of all the cuts and the wound on her head.

The paramedics reassure me the entire flight to OU Medical Center that Rosie is going to be fine. I'm not allowed to be with her as they are checking her over. She has to have a CT to check the wound on her head. We aren't sure what she was hit with; the wound took fifteen stitches to close. She has numerous stitches over her body to close the slices Paula inflicted on her.

Macy and David arrive as I'm waiting on the doctor to come out and let me know how she is. "Mike, is she all, right?" Macy runs to me crying.

"Detective Anderson?" A man dressed in scrubs comes out of the double doors.

"That's me. How is Rosie?" Macy, David and I all gather around him.

"We had to clean the wound before we could close it. There were wood particles embedded in her skull. The rest of the liaisons weren't that bad, only a few that were deep. The blade that was used was very sharp." He looks at me. "I hope you got the person that did this to her. She is going to have physiological trauma that is going to need to be treated long after her wounds heal."

"Can I see her?" Macy asks.

"For tonight, I think one visitor is all she needs. She is asking for you, Detective."

"Macy, I'll call you later and let you know how she's doing." I give her a hug.

"Tell her we love her."

Giving her another comforting hug, I say, "I will."

The doctor and I walk through the double doors. I glance back to see Macy crying in David's arms. "She's right in here."

I look in the window and see Rosie curled into the fetal position, facing away from the door. I knock gently, so I don't scare her. At first, she doesn't move.

I slowly enter the room in case she has fallen asleep. "Rosie, it's Mike. Can I sit with you?" Her shoulders shake slightly as I round the bed. "Rosie, honey, you're safe now." I reach out to place my hand on her arm.

When my skin touches hers, she shivers gently. She looks at me with so much pain in her eyes. I sit on the edge of the bed next to her, and she climbs into my lap, wrapping her arms around my neck. Taking a blanket off the end of the bed, I carry her to the chair in the corner, where I sit down while holding her.

She doesn't say anything, just curls into my chest and cries.

I rub her back, holding her tight, reminding her, over and over, that she's safe. I won't let anyone hurt her again. After an hour or so, the tears stop falling and her breathing becomes shallow as she has fallen to sleep.

A few hours later, a nurse comes in, wanting to wake her to check Rosie's vitals. I tell her to leave. "Thank you," I hear Rosie softly whisper in my ear. "Thank you for finding me."

"I'll always find you," I whisper back to her.

* * *

Morning comes around, and Rosie is still in my lap, wrapped in my arms; we hear the door open slightly, and I tighten my protective hold on her.

"Have you been in that chair all night?" my sister asks, concern in her face.

Rosie tries to jump free of my embrace. "My gawd, your legs have to be killing you."

I won't let her free. "My legs are just fine. Sit still before you injure another part of my anatomy."

This causes a giggle to escape from Rosie. "Do you want me to get up?"

David takes Macy by the elbow and pulls her toward the door. "Let's go get them some coffee and something to eat. Hospital food is never very good. We'll be right back, you two." He winks at me before dragging Macy out of the room.

"Honestly, Mike, let me get off your lap. Your legs have to be dead asleep," Macy says.

"I'm not ready to let you go yet, Rosie. I'm so sorry this

happened to you. I should have seen that she…" I stop, unsure how to continue.

"Paula was a fucking lunatic. Is that what you were going to say?"

"That works."

"It's not your fault. This is all on her. You couldn't have known any of this was going to happen." She runs her fingers through my hair. "I went with her willingly. I… I thought we were going on a date. I never imagined I was in danger until it was too late." I rub my hand down her back as she talks. "I knew you would find me, just like you did Macy."

"I don't think I can let you go, even for a little while." I brush her hair out of her face. "You are so beautiful."

The door opens, and this time, it's a nurse with the doctor. "I see you're feeling better. Can you come back over and sit on the bed so I can check you out and see about getting you out of here this morning."

"That sounds perfect," Rosie agrees and gently stands, walking over to the bed, still holding my hand.

Fifteen minutes later, she has a clean bill of health with a minor concussion and orders to take it easy for the next few days. We call Macy and David to tell them to meet us at the house for breakfast instead of coming back to the hospital.

Macy had brought some sweats, T-shirt, and shoes for Rosie to put on and left them inside the door in a chair. I called an Uber to pick us up and take us home. When we arrived, Macy came running out of the house to pull Rosie into her arms. "Thank gawd you're home safe. Don't think about arguing. You're staying with us until your well or forever."

I sweep her off her feet, carrying her into the house.

"Who's going to argue?" Rosie asks, placing her head on my chest. I set her on the couch.

"Are you comfortable here, or would you rather be upstairs in the bedroom?"

"Here is good for now. You're not leaving, are you?" Rosie asks with a tinge of panic in her voice.

"I'm not going anywhere." I sit down next to her. She instantly climbs onto my lap.

"Don't leave me. Not yet?" She buries her face in my neck.

"Rosie, honey, I need you to look at me." She slowly raises up and looks at me. "I may have to go to the station in the next few days and so will you to answer questions, but I will always come back to you as long as you want me." I cup her face between my hands. "I have feelings for you, and I would like to see where this goes between us." I kiss her lips gently and all around her face.

"You have feelings for me?" She sits up straight on my lap and looks at me. "That does make sleeping in your bed so much more convenient getting to know each other."

"Rosie, the doctor said you have to rest and take it easy for a few days." I realize the next few days are going to be very stressful for me. She kisses me. Not a kiss of someone that is a friend. A kiss of someone craving me, desperate to get as close to me as possible.

"I'm yours, Mike. Forever and always."

The End.

EPILOGUE

MIKE

It's been over a year since Rosie was kidnapped by Paula. We have been sharing her apartment ever since she healed from her injuries. I have been clean since my first N.A. meeting, where I ran into Rosie. We both still go to meetings and help others when we can. I'm still in the Narcotics Division, I just don't do undercover work anymore. I spend a lot of time at the gym helping David work with the kids. This is where I find a lot of my joy.

Rosie and Macy have even started working with some of the kids a couple of days a week, giving art classes at the tattoo shop. Even more officers help out now. David has thirty kids a semester signed up for different classes.

I have a big surprise planned for Rosie this morning. She and Macy are supposed to meet David and me at the diner for breakfast. We try to do this at least once a week.

David and I are on the way to the diner to meet the girls. "Are you getting nervous?' He asks me as I check my pocket again to make sure the little velvet box is in it.

"Maybe I should do it in private?" I look at him.

"The diner is the perfect place; besides, we all have history here."

We arrive before the girls do, so I go in the back to talk to the cook and waitress while David goes to our favorite booth in the back.

I sit down at the booth as they walk in the door. The waitress comes with coffee for the four of us. Instead of taking our order at that time, she walks back to the kitchen. A few minutes later, she comes out with a tray full of food. Omelets for David and me, a plate of pancakes is handed to Macy, and another plate of pancakes is handed to me to give to Rosie.

On top of the pancakes in a pillow of Cool Whip is a sapphire engagement ring. Macy's eyes go wide when she sees the ring. Rosie is taking a sip of her coffee when she looks at Macy.

"What is wrong with…" Her eyes fall on the plate I'm holding and the ring in the center. Her hand flies to her mouth.

The entire diner has gone silent. "Rosie, you have filled a void I didn't realize I had in my life. This last year has been amazing with you in it. I want to build a lifetime of memories with you. Will you marry me?"

She doesn't say anything as tears flow down her cheeks. She just begins to nod her head in agreement. Then finally she says it, "Yes, yes of course, I'll marry you."

The entire diner breaks out into cheers as we kiss.

I finally have everything I've ever wanted in life. My family, someone that loves me as much as I love her.

The End.

ABOUT THE AUTHOR

Nancy's a wild child trapped inside a responsible adult. She found a release for my fun-loving disobedient self in writing. She loves tequila, dragons, and wizards. She has a collection of the mythical creatures that decorate her office. She finally allowed herself the time to go after her dream of writing. Her characters are stubborn, strong, full of emotion and cuss like sailors. (Just like her.)

Nancy has always had an interest in paranormal. Reading anything and everything she can on the subject of psychics and mediums. The theory that the average human only uses ten percent of their brain has always led her to wonder: What's a person capable of if they tapped into the other ninety percent?

She enjoys meeting new people and spending time with them discussing books. If you see her online or in person, be sure and say hello.

ALSO BY NANCY CHASTAIN

Deadly Obsessions Series:

Obsession Book #1

Betrayal Book #2

Sacrifice Book #3 coming soon

Other

Find Me

Caged Rage

Saving Charly

Beast

Honor Thy Father

Deceptive Castings

Made in the USA
Coppell, TX
22 May 2022